Hattie's Pink House

Hattie's Pink House

A novel by S.R. Doss

G
W
B
Golden Word Books
Santa Fe, NM

Library of Congress Control Number 2020932828

G
W
B

Printed in the United States of America

Published by Golden Word Books, Santa Fe, New Mexico.

ISBN 978-1-948749-58-9

Hattie's Pink House

GONE WITH THE WIND

ON A SUN BAKED TEXAS AFTERNOON A THIN, MIDDLE AGED woman walked north across the Colorado River bridge in downtown Austin, wearing pink high-heeled slippers and holding a pink parasol above her head. Halfway across the bridge she stopped, leaned against the sidewalk railing and watched two policemen directing traffic, while a maintenance crew cleared broken pavement from the bridge.

One of the officers saw the woman and smiled. When she nodded he turned away from the work crew and approached her. They talked for a moment. She pointed to the state capitol, a mile away on Congress Avenue. Then she held the parasol to her side, opened her purse behind it, and handed him an envelope. The policeman counted the money in the envelope, put it in his pocket and went back to guiding traffic.

As the cars heading south slowed down and came to a stop, waiting to enter the lane still open, the woman stared at a yellow Cadillac convertible with the top down. She lit a cigarette and watched to see who the driver might be. After a moment she looked back as the Cadillac drove on. She leaned against a railing on the bridge, smiled, finished the cigarette, and walked on.

The driver of the convertible watched for a speed limit sign, turned on the car radio, felt the wind in his face, straightened his sunglasses, and pulled down on his Army overseas cap. Unlike the woman on the bridge he was young, in his early twenties, a second lieutenant wearing a summer uniform with parachute wings on his blouse and an Eighty Second Airborne patch on the left shoulder.

The lieutenant sped up when he saw the city limits, grunting as he listened to a news broadcast from Washington, the announcer pointing out that today marks the fourteenth anniversary of America dropping the atom bomb on Hiroshima, and President Eisenhower is playing golf while thousands march outside the White House, pleading for a ban on atomic weapons.

"Cowards" he muttered. "Crawl back in your damn fallout shelters. And take this announcer with you." He turned off the radio and drove on for a mile on US 81, a two-lane highway heading south to San Antonio. After another mile he stopped on the side of the road, opened the glove compartment and unfolded a map. Glancing at the map he looked back for traffic and turned around, driving slowly.

When he reached the city limit sign again he parked at a roadside clearing, got out of the Cadillac, and gazed at an open field across the highway. He stood there, looking at the map, turning around to look at the trees behind him, then again at the empty field, and once again at the Austin city limit sign. "I'll be damned" he muttered. "It's gone, they did it, they moved the city limits on her."

The lieutenant spread the map on the hood of the car, looked across the highway, then back at the map, and grunted again. After a moment he folded the map, opened a thermos bottle and poured beer in a cup. He took off his cap, removed his sunglasses and rubbed sweat from his face, sipping beer and looking across the highway as a station wagon drove into the clearing and parked next to his car.

A young girl got out. And then a man, older than the lieutenant, hobbling to the rear of the station wagon. Rubbing the side of his face, where a deep scar ran down from his left eye to his jaw. He opened the rear of the station wagon and the girl fastened a leash on a Doberman, letting the dog piddle against a tire. Paying no attention to the dog, she stared at the lieutenant, seeming puzzled.

"Is that Audie Murphy?" she asked. "He sure looks like him."

"He sure does" said the man. "But that's not him. Audie's not in the Army any more, he's making cowboy movies." The girl shrugged her shoulders and led the dog into the trees. The man followed her. When he returned he looked at the convertible, stood behind the lieutenant, and frowned.

"Quite a car" said the man. "They Army must pay well these days if you can drive one like that, a brand new Cadillac."

"Not new" the lieutenant replied. "It's a nineteen fifty five. Been in storage four years." Still sipping beer he walked around to the driver's side, ready to leave.

"Wait" said the man. "I've seen you some place before." As he spoke he moved closer, squinting his eyes and rubbing the scar on his face.

"I wouldn't know" said the lieutenant. "But you won't see me around here long. I'm headed for Germany."

He got in the Cadillac, heard the Doberman growling, saw the girl coming from the trees with her dog, and pointed across the highway. "Turn him loose in that field over there, it's empty now" he said, loud enough for her to hear.

She watched as he started the engine and drove to the road stop exit, waiting for traffic to pass by.

"Who was that?" she asked. "Did you know him in the war?"

"Not in my war" the man answered. "He's too young for that."

"Who was he, then?" she asked.

"Little sister, I don't know" he answered. "I'm trying to place him."

They got in the station wagon, the girl in the back seat with the dog, the man behind the steering wheel, talking to himself. "That face" he said. "I saw it somewhere, in the papers, on TV, some kind of scandal, damn it."

"A scandal, what about?" asked the girl.

"He was in some kind of trouble" the man answered, rubbing the scar on his face again. "But damn it, I just can't remember what it was."

"He had a pretty car" said the girl. "When I grow up I'd like to have a car like that." She was petting the dog, trying to keep it from growling. The man turned his head and looked back at her.

"When you grow up" he said. "Like the girls who worked across the highway."

"In that field? What did they do? Pick cotton?"

"Not cotton, little sister. You won't get a car like that by picking cotton."

He started the engine of the station wagon, turned the radio on, dialed in some music, and muttered "That lieutenant, damn it, where did I see him before?" By then the Cadillac was gone, heading back to Austin.

The lieutenant saw the bridge had been cleared, drove across the river, and stopped at the corner of Congress and Sixth Street. He parked in front of a store where the sign said Herman's Beer and Liquors, got out of his car, and looked up at the sign. After a moment he straightened his uniform, stomped the dust off his paratrooper boots, and entered, standing inside the doorway and looking around.

A man with an apron around his waist was standing on a stool behind the counter, reaching for a quart of whiskey. He came down, put the bottle in a paper sack, handed it to a couple, and placed money in a cash register as they walked away. When he saw the lieutenant he took off his apron and came from behind the counter, grinning as he greeted him, shaking hands and speaking with a German accent.

"Wie gehts, Phillip" he said. "I heard you were back. How long has it been?"

"Nearly five years" said the lieutenant. "How'd you know I'm in town?"

"Hattie came by a while ago, she said she saw you."

"Hattie? Well, hell, Herman, here I am, Second Lieutenant Phillip Dee, United States Army, at your service." He clicked his heels and saluted. Herman raised his arm in an old fashioned Nazi salute, still grinning.

"Ja wohl" said Herman. "What about the University, your degree, I heard you. . ."

"After I got fired I finished, needed some correspondence courses, but. . ."

"Fired. What Black did to you wasn't right."

"Screw it, Herman. So Hattie said she saw me? Where?"

"When you were going across the bridge, driving that Cadillac you won."

"Right, it took several months of jump pay to get it out of storage."

"She said tell you to kiss off, you owe her a letter."

"I brought her a present instead. What happened to her house? It's gone."

"The Pink House. It's gone, all right. But most of the men who come in here, they remember, they smile when they see that."

Herman pointed to a painting on the wall behind the counter, huge, three feet wide, showing a woman dressed like Scarlett O'Hara, holding a pink parasol above her head, with a pink purse hanging at her side, standing in front of what looked like a small scale replica of Tara, the mansion in the movie *Gone With The Wind.*

Dee looked at the painting and frowned. "A land mark" he said. "That's what I told the City Council. You remember, they wouldn't listen."

"After you left, they wouldn't listen last year, either" said Herman.

"So what did they do? Move the city limits to close her down?"

"Not close her down, they passed a tax on her business. A big open meeting in the City Courthouse, you should have heard what Hattie told them, she said. . ."

Herman held a hand over his mouth, breaking off in mid sentence as a woman came through the door. Dee turned and looked. Middle aged, no lipstick, dressed in a business suit, carrying a briefcase, and angry about something.

"I don't get it" she said to Herman. "I ordered a Scotch and soda at my hotel and they told me I should come over here first."

"Yes ma'am" said Herman. "What kind of Scotch would you like?"

"The kind they serve at a bar" she answered. "You people have some damned strange rules in Texas."

"Lady, where are you from?" he asked.

"Washington D.C. What difference does that make?"

"Down here, they can serve you ice and soda, but you have to have your own bottle. That's what these paper sacks are for."

"I'm supposed to carry a bottle around in a sack? Like hell I will. Give me a pint of that, I can fit it in my briefcase." She pointed to a row of bottles on a shelf next to the painting and turned to Dee as she waited.

"That picture you're looking at, lieutenant, what's that?" she asked.

"Lady, believe it or not, that used to be a famous bawdy house" he answered.

"Bawdy house? You mean a whore house. This whole state is a whore house."

She handed Herman a five dollar bill, put the bottle in her briefcase, along with the change he handed her, and left. Dee watched, smiling, and then looked at Herman when he heard him laughing.

"That's what Hattie told them" said Herman. "The City Council, when they levied that tax on her girls, she said this whole state's a whore house."

"Too bad I missed it" said Dee. "Sounds like a hell of a story."

"Your paper had to water it down. She told them right in public, her girls fucked for her, not for a bunch of shithead politicians."

"So what did they do? Throw her in jail?"

"Not Hattie. She said go screw yourselves, she'd sell the house and close it down before she'd give them a penny. She did, she closed it."

"Herman, what are you telling me? The city tore it down then?"

"No, after she sold it, that was only the start. Wait a minute, I'll tell you what happened."

Herman went to the door, locked it, and flipped a card that said Closed, Back in Fifteen Minutes. He opened a cooler then, brought out two cans of beer, and handed one to Dee, laughing so hard he spewed foam on the counter when he pulled the tab from his can and raised it to his mouth.

"The real estate company that bought it, they were the ones who had to tear it down" said Herman. "They couldn't find a family who would stay there."

"A land mark, right" said Dee. "I can guess what happened."

"The first people they sold it to, some rich people from Utah, the company fixed it up, painted it white, put in a new gravel driveway, new drapes, even."

"Utah. Mormons. How long did they last?"

"One month. They couldn't take it, all night long, drunks banging on the door, yelling let me in, don't tell me this ain't a whore house, I been here."

"The police, they couldn't stop it?"

"Hell no, they wouldn't go near, they were pissed off at the City Council."

"One month. So who bought it then?"

"A big family from Wisconsin, just moving here, six kids, they couldn't take it either. One month. And the price had gone down, way down, Phil."

"One month, six kids who couldn't sleep, with all that banging on the door, damn, Herman, I'm surprised they lasted that long."

"The last family, a man from back East some place, he'd heard things were cheap in Texas, he thought it was a bargain. By then it was, the real estate company was trying to dump it. That's when it got worse, Phil, the night they moved in."

"Worse? How could it get any worse?"

"He had a wife and two grown daughters, that's how."

"Whoops, two grown daughters. Herman, are you making this up?"

"Hell no, it was one of the daughters who fired the shotgun that night."

Herman was laughing so hard he was almost choking. Dee patted him on the shoulder, raised Herman's beer to his mouth and made him swallow, trying to calm him down. Herman shoved the beer aside and went on laughing.

"All right" said Dee. "What's this about a shotgun? What happened?"

"One of the daughters was on the porch when a half dozen cars drove in. The Baylor football team, the night they finished spring training."

"Baptists looking to get laid. They thought it was a whore house still?"

"Hell yes, they were drunk before they left Waco, they grabbed her on the porch and tried to screw her right there. That's when the other one came out with the shotgun."

"She fired, you said. Anybody get hurt?"

"No, but they drove off so fast one of them rolled his car on the highway."

"The police, Herman, they must have gone out there for that."

"Not even then. No charges were ever filed. That family moved out the same night, they never unpacked, they left town the next day."

"Not very happy with Austin. I can see why."

"Happy? The Texas football coach sure was. The whole damned Baylor backfield was in that car that rolled over. They're out for the season."

Herman was still laughing as he went to the door, unlocked it, and flipped the card to Open For Business. Dee pushed his beer away and waited, shaking his head, no longer laughing.

"The city finally made them tear it down" said Herman. "The real estate company took a bath on that one."

"A car wreck" said Dee. "Too bad."

"The police chief told me about it" said Herman. "What went on out there, he damned near had a nervous breakdown over that."

Dee leaned against the counter, saying nothing. Silent, looking down, gritting his teeth. Herman watched for a moment, then came around the counter, stood beside him, and patted him on the shoulder.

"What's wrong, Phil? A minute ago, when I told you what happened, hell, you were laughing like me."

"It's that car wreck you mentioned, Herman. That reminded me of something I'm trying to forget."

"We all have plenty to forget. What is it?"

"At Fort Bragg, a woman I got involved with."

"Women. You never had much luck with women."

"No, but her, damn it, I asked her to marry me."

"She told you to kiss off? So what?"

"A general's daughter. The man I work for, that's how I met her."

Herman grunted. "A general" he muttered. "In my army you would not have dared." Dee was not listening. He was looking down at the counter, speaking softly, almost to himself.

"The night I asked her, she said she loved me, but."

"But? But what?"

"But she hated second lieutenants, she'd never marry one."

"She told you no? So that was it?"

"That was it, all right. She drove away drunk and hit a truck head on."

"Damn, Phil, I'm sorry. I shouldn't have. . ."

"C'est la vie, Herman. That's French for fuck it."

Herman looked at Dee, then stepped behind the counter and reached up on a shelf. "Here's the best way to forget it" he said, and brought down a bottle of Ancient Age bourbon. Dee grunted, shaking his head as he looked at the bottle.

"Ancient Age" he said. "Damn, we used to drink that by the barrel."

"The good old days, Phil. If you and your buddies had kept that up, hell, by now I'd be as rich as Hattie."

"But not as rich as that sonofabitch who owns the paper."

"No where near. That television station he owns now, that's a gold mine."

Dee clinched his fists on top the counter. Shaking his head again, a disgusted look on his face. For a moment they were silent, both of them, Herman waiting, as if he knew what was coming next.

"Lomax, so he got the TV station for him. One crooked bastard, Herman."

"I know, but he keeps getting elected. The paper sees to that."

"I had him nailed. You remember, Hattie showed me how to get him."

"I remember. Sure, she knew where the voting records were."

"Lomax, damn it, he should have gone to prison."

"So they fired you instead. Forget it, Phil, that's the kind of shit that happens."

"That's worse than shit, being fired so the owner of a paper could get rich."

"He's rich, all right. They're moving to a new building by the river."

Dee shook his head again and reached in his pocket. "Screw their new building" he said. "Here's the key for the Cadillac, Herman. Take it for a drive if you like, I'm going up the hill and see where I used to work."

A block away, at the corner of Sixth and Colorado, Dee watched as men in coveralls loaded trucks parked next to the building there. "They're moving the linotype machines" he muttered to himself. "I fed a lot of copy into those damned things." As one of the trucks pulled away he went down to the basement, looking around to see what was left.

On one side of the room a man moved a forklift up a ramp leading out to the street, hauling crates and boxes. On the other side, two men stood next to a row of steel cabinets, opening drawers, sorting through pieces of metal, setting some aside, throwing the rest in a barrel.

One of the men turned around to wipe his face and saw Dee. "Hey, Dummy, look who's here" he yelled at the other man and tapped him on the shoulder. They were older than Dee, both their faces were scarred, and the one named Dummy was limping as they approached him.

"Jake, you too, Dummy, how the hell are you?" Dee asked and shook hands.

"How long's it been?" Jake asked, "Four, five years? We got your letters from Fort Bragg, what brings you back, Phil?"

"You remember that Cadillac I won? The one I left here when I joined up."

Jake turned to Dummy and yelled. "You hear what he said? That car, the one he won in the raffle, with that dollar from Charlie Black, remember?"

"That bastard Black" said Dee. "Herman told me he's rich now."

Jake nodded and walked back to the steel cabinets. "Come over here" he yelled to Dummy, pointing to the barrel. "Look for the column plates we stuck in there."

Dee watched as Dummy grunted, leaned down and rummaged around in the barrel, while Jake yelled "Look for Dee's plate" in his ears. After a moment Dummy stood up and handed a piece of metal to Jake, who smiled as he handed it to Dee.

"I'll be damned" said Dee. "That's what got me in all the trouble." He looked at it and shook his head. A metal plate two columns wide, with the words *THE BLOTTER* in italic type, and below it, in smaller type, Police Reports By Phillip Dee.

"Yeah" said Jake. "Black told us to melt it down, the day after he fired you, but we never did."

"Melt it down. No wonder. All because of that bastard Lomax."

"Fuck Lomax" said Jake. "You had him nailed. Everybody knew it."

"Sure. Hattie knew where the voting records were, but. . ."

"Hattie. Her place is gone. Phil. They tore down the Pink House."

"I know, Herman told me about it. She came by his place a while ago."

"You and Jack and Steve, you three were her best customers."

"Hell yes" said Dee. "Only place we could get a drink at two in the morning."

"A drink, my ass" Jake laughed. "I asked Hattie one time if Jack kept his hat on when he banged one of her girls. All she did was wink."

"That hat of his. Hell, Jake, that's how all that crap got started."

Dee wiped the plate with a handkerchief and put it in his pocket. He was silent for a moment, looking around the room, looking at the concrete squares where the linotypes had been, at the barrel filled with trash, then back at Jake and Dummy.

"Crap is right" said Jake. "You were screwed. So Black could cover for Lomax."

"Screwed, sure" said Dee. "Not a damned thing I could do but run for cover."

"A real mess after you left. Black had to bust his ass to make it look like you were some kind of crooked reporter, he even. . ."

"Well, hell, so I'm a soldier now. You know, Jake, it's because of all those stories you told me I went airborne."

"Normandy, damned right. Nothing like a night drop, Phil."

"Sainte-Mère-Église. Maybe when I get overseas I'll see what it looks like."

"It looked nice when we jumped in. After that, hell, I wouldn't know."

"Dummy, he's never been able to talk about it, has he?"

"Not a word, deaf, too, after that satchel charge went off behind us."

"He's a damned good printer, Jake. Take care of him."

"He's fine. You know why? He can't hear all the shit that goes on around here."

Dummy had gone back to work, throwing junk in the barrel. Jake wrote something on a sheet of paper and handed it to him.

Dummy read it, scribbled a reply, looked at Dee, and held his fingers up, the airborne signal to hook up and get ready to jump. He was smiling, and so was Dee when he read what Dummy had written.

"You see what I told him" said Jake. "How we were talking about Normandy."

"Dummy, he's damned near killed after you jumped, and you see what he wrote me? Airborne! Stand in the door!"

"Hell yes, Phil. They screwed you, but you've made out fine."

Dee looked around the basement one last time, at the side where the printing presses had been, at the rolling tables where the type had been set in pages, at the corner where the galley proofs had been made. After a moment he shook hands, with Dummy first, with Jake second.

"Look" he said. "I'm parked at Herman's. When you two finish work, go down there, you'll find a couple of bottles of sour mash waiting for you."

Then he told them he would write from Germany and saluted, and when they returned the salute he turned around and walked down the hill, back to Herman's.

The Cadillac was no longer where he left it. Dee saw it on the other side of Sixth Street, parked in front of the Driskill Hotel. He went to it, removed his dog tags from his neck, took the spare key off the chain, unlocked the trunk, unzipped his B4 bag, and took a gift wrapped package from it.

He looked at his watch. Only a few more hours of daylight. "Time to get rolling" he said out loud, and went into Herman's.

A man and a woman were standing at the counter, watching Herman stuff wads of crumpled newspapers around a dozen bottles in a case of wine. "Six Beaujolais, six Chiantis" he said. "Fourteen dollars."

The women looked at the man she was with and frowned. "A foreigner" she said. "The way he pronounced Beaujolais, another asshole foreigner." Herman handed the man his change and answered, "No ma'am, I'm from New Mexico."

As they walked past him to the door, with the man holding the case of wine in his arms, Dee heard the woman grumble "New Mexico, my ass, he doesn't look like a pepper belly Mexican to me."

Herman paid no attention. He was busy trying to flatten one of the crumpled sheets left over, part of a newspaper yellow with age.

"She's right" said Dee. "You need a sombrero."

"That woman's dumb" said Herman, looking up from the paper. "Before you came in, she looked at that picture of Hattie's, you know what she said? It reminded her of Old Santa Fe."

"So you told her off. Herman, it's a wonder you stay in business."

"Three years in a POW camp there, I've been in Santa Fe."

Dee put a ten dollar bill on the counter, placed a hand on top the paper, and pointed to a shelf holding Jack Daniel's whisky. "To hell with her" he said. "Jake will be by in a while. With Dummy. Give them two bottles of Old Number Seven."

Herman looked up from the paper. "Jake" he said. "You know what he calls me? The Gauleiter of the Rio Grande."

"No wonder, the way you made out. How's Lucille?"

"In Albuquerque, seeing her mother. Here's a postcard she sent me."

Dee looked at the postcard. "I still think that should have been printed" he said. "That piece I wrote about you two. POWs planting crops for Americans, after the war one of the Germans comes back and marries a lady he met in a cornfield, that's a damned good story. Not good enough for Buck. He wouldn't run it."

"You know why Phil, you heard what that woman said just now. Buck was right, not good for my business, letting people know I was in the Wehrmacht."

"Buck. A hell of a managing editor, Herman. Gave me all kinds of shit when I first started. You ever see him?"

"He comes by when he's in town. Here's one he did print."

Herman straightened the crumpled sheet and moved it around so Dee could see it. He looked at the date of the paper. Monday, June 7, 1954. "Hell, Herman, that's five years ago. What about it?"

"I keep a pile of old papers in the back room, right?"

"Sure, to wrap bottles. So?"

"All trash, and look what I found. Here, have a can of beer. Look at the other side, see if you remember."

Dee turned the paper over and saw the picture on the front page. A crowd of D-Day veterans in the lobby of the Driskill Hotel, shaking hands with Lyndon Johnson and the Governor of Texas. Beneath it, a two column headline. Normandy Heroes Celebrate With Tales Of Valor.

And below the headline, a story with the byline Phillip Dee.

"I remember, all right" he said. "Most of all, how Buck got on my ass when I came in that afternoon."

He sat down in a chair next to the counter and looked at the metal plate Jake had given him. The Blotter. Sipping from the can of beer, reading through the paper Herman had found. Remembering. The tenth anniversary of D-Day, the celebration, the story he had written.

Remembering. Grunting and remembering. . .

CHEERLEADERS

"PHIL, YOU PISS ANT, SEE WHAT IT SAYS ON MY CAP? BUCK Hooper, U.S. Navy. Come into my office, so I can chew your ass out."

Dee followed him through the door with the words Managing Editor on it, watching as Buck stepped behind his desk, with his back turned, staring at a half dozen pictures of Navy ships on the wall. Forty years old at most, built like a middleweight boxer, growling as he looked at the pictures and then turned around.

"Alice, the town of Alice, you know where that is, Dee?"

"Down in the valley, Buck, near Kingsville, what about it?"

"You ever read the weather page?"

"The weather page? Sometimes, sure, but. . ."

"Look at this headline, tell me what you think."

Buck folded the morning paper to the weather page, grunted, and handed the paper across his desk, pointing to a two column headline, black, with a kicker above it. Dee smiled as he read it:

Texas Rainfall
ALICE GETS.
SIX INCHES

"What do I think, Buck? I'd say Lulu strikes again."

"Those idiots on the night desk, how do you think this got past them, Dee?"

"I don't know, maybe they were half asleep, maybe. . ."

"Maybe they're as dumb as she is, maybe they're as dumb as you are."

"Look, Buck, Lulu was in the Navy, I know, that's why you keep her around, but what's this all about? What do you mean, you want to chew my ass out?"

Buck took the paper from Dee, folded it back to the front page, shook his head, sat down in his swivel chair and turned around, looking at the Navy pictures on the wall, pointing to one, speaking without looking at Dee.

"See that?" he asked. "What does that look like?"

"A battleship, maybe" said Dee. "How would I know?"

"This one, what does this look like?"

"Look, I haven't had much sleep. What do you mean, chew my ass out?"

"How many ships do you think the Navy had at Normandy?"

"A hundred? Two hundred. A thousand, for all I know. So what?"

"How many goddamned sailors were there?"

"Sailors? How many sailors? Buck, what the hell's eating you?"

Buck turned around and reached for the paper again. Growling, leaning across his desk, holding the front page in Dee's face. "That headline" he said. "You see what it says? D-Day veterans celebrate with tales of valor."

"You want a better one?" asked Dee. "I didn't write that headline, you know that."

"To hell with the headline, you wrote the story."

"I did. Interviews, like you told me."

"How many did you talk to?"

"Twenty, twenty five maybe. I used the best quotes I had, I. . ."

"Eight. You wrote about eight D-Day vets. All Army. Not one damned sailor."

Dee took the paper from Buck, glanced at the front page, and looked up at the Navy pictures on the wall. "So that's it" he said. "That's what you're pissed off about. I left out your sailors."

"You did" said Buck. "Now get the hell out of my office."

"Not yet" said Dee. "I talked to a few, one of them told me he hated the Navy, it made him seasick. You think I should have used that quote?"

"No. Go away, leave me alone."

"Here's something better. One of your sailors talked about Lyndon Johnson. You want to hear what he said?"

"Senator Johnson? I don't think so. All right, what did he say?"

"He said he knew about Johnson, he's a phony, he served in the Navy, all he was doing was setting himself up for his next campaign when the war was over."

"That's crap. Nothing but drunk talk."

"Maybe, but a great quote, Buck. So get off my butt about the Navy."

"Sit down" said Buck. "How long has it been since I hired you?"

"How long? Two years next month."

"You're still at the University. When are you going to finish?"

"A year, maybe, if I get enough sleep to pass my courses. Why?"

"I'm moving you to the police beat" said Buck. "So you can get some sleep and pass your goddamned courses, so you can graduate and go some place else. Now leave me alone."

Buck turned around in his swivel chair, looking at the Navy pictures. Dee waited, then walked out, back to the city room, looking at the other reporters coming to work. Three in the afternoon, if his watch was right.

"The police beat" he mumbled out loud. "So I can get some sleep, Buck says. Sleep? What the hell is that? And who gives a damn about Lulu? That's his problem."

At well past two in the morning Dee unlocked the door to an upstairs apartment on Loraine Street, turned on the lights, saw no one else was there, walked past the bar in the living room, and went to the kitchen to make instant coffee.

As the kettle of water he placed on a stove started to percolate he yawned, opened a cabinet, and searched for a cup. None there.

He looked in the sink, piled with dirty dishes. When he found a cup he rinsed it and waited for the water to boil.

"A goddamn pig pen" he said out loud, looking down at the sink. "We ought to hire someone to clean this place."

Water spilled over the cup when he poured from the kettle. Dee looked down at the mess on the kitchen counter, wiped the counter with a paper towel, and walked away, taking the coffee with him to a bedroom in the hallway.

When he entered the bedroom he saw the light was still on, the fan on a windowsill was still running, and a textbook with a blue cover was still on his bed where he had left it. He put the cup on his desk, sat down, reached for the book, and groaned as he looked at the title. Conversational French for Beginners.

A note inside reminded him where to start. Page 19 for Wednesday.

"Où est la bibliothèque?" he read out loud, pronouncing the words slowly. "A bibliothèque, what's that? A Bible salesman? No, hell, look it up." In the back of the book he found the translation. "Où est la bibliothèque, where is the library? Sure, if I'm ever in Paris that's the first thing I'll ask for, the damned library."

He stood up, stretched, took off his clothes, and sat at the desk, wearing only a pair of shorts, letting the breeze from the fan cool his face, sipping coffee, reading French out loud, trying to memorize what the words meant in English.

"Je suis Américain." I am American. "Où est la gare?" Where is the train station?

"Où est le restaurant?" Where is the restaurant?

"Qu'est-ce que vous prenez?" What would you like?

"Je n'ai pas très faim." I am not very hungry.

"Je suis . . . je suis . . . je . . ."

Dee snapped his head back as he started to doze off. One more sentence was enough. He turned off his desk lamp and pushed the book away, staggered to his bed and fell face down, sound asleep in a matter of seconds.

Asleep, but only for a moment.

"Get up, you need a drink" came a sound from somewhere. Loud. Dee did not move. When the light went on he sat up, rubbed his eyes and looked. "What happened to your suit?" he asked. "You look like shit, Steve."

"Hattie, that's what she said." Drunken words from a tall and gangly figure with a glass in his hand. Leaning against the doorway. Wearing a white linen suit with one sleeve ripped loose. Mumbling. "She said Parker, you and Galloway, where's your buddy Dee, he could have helped you."

"Help you do what?" asked Dee. "What the hell have you two been up to?" No answer. Dee crawled out of bed and followed him to the bar in the living room, where Parker was pouring another drink.

In the corner, Galloway sat slumped in a chair. Bald, with the light shining on his head, holding a straw hat in his lap, a hat that looked crushed and run over. With a drink in his hand, staring up at the ceiling.

"Jack, what happened to your hat?" asked Dee.

"The mayor stepped on it" said Galloway.

"Phil, old buddy, put some clothes on" said Parker. "Have a drink."

"Drink, hell" said Dee. "What's this about the mayor?"

"Damned Aggie lover" muttered Galloway. He stood up, threw his hat on the floor, finished his drink, set his glass on the bar, and stumbled into the hallway, heading for a bedroom. Mumbling "Damned Aggie lover" as he disappeared.

Dee turned to Parker. "Steve, what's this crap about the mayor? What happened at Hattie's?"

"You have a sewing kit?" asked Parker.

"There's one in my bedroom" said Dee. "What happened to your sleeve?"

"The mayor" said Parker. "What are you doing without any clothes on?"

"You woke me up, damn it. I've been trying to study, I have a class at seven."

"Piss on your class" said Parker, leaning against the bar. "The mayor, too. Where's your sewing kit?"

"The top drawer in my bureau" Dee answered. "I'll be there in a minute." He took the empty glasses from the bar, set them on the pile in the sink, and went to his room. When he got there Parker was lying on his bed. Snoring, sound asleep with his suit on.

Dee started to wake him up, but he looked at his watch and shook his head. "Hell, why bother" he mumbled. "I might as well dress and get to class a little early. Then, hell, I have to meet my folks for lunch. It's going to be a long damned day."

He looked at Galloway's hat in the corner. Crushed. "Hattie's" he muttered. "God only knows what happened this time."

Dawn was breaking as Dee entered the classroom where his French course met. Empty, except for a janitor cleaning chalkboards and opening windows. He took a seat on the last row of tables in the rear of the room, opened his textbook, and started reading out loud the assignment for today.

"Où est la bibliothèque?" Where is the library?

"Où est la gare?" Where is the train station?

"Je suis Américain." I am an American.

In the front of the room the janitor climbed on a stool, looked at his watch, and adjusted the clock above the chalkboard. Almost twenty minutes until seven, Dee noticed.

He yawned and put his head down on his book. Ready to speak in French when the class starts. The French word for the damn library. Or whatever. Just make it to seven fifty when this class is over and get some sleep then.

He raised his head when he heard voices. Twenty or thirty students had taken their places in the classroom. With a new instructor, it looked like. In front of him, all alone on the next to last row of tables, a coed with bright red hair held her hand up and answered a question.

"Mi casa es su casa" she said. "My house is your house."

In the front of the room a coed said something Dee could not hear. The instructor stepped forward and patted her on the head, evidently telling her to speak louder. She was close to yelling when she spoke again.

"Quisiera una habitación con baño" she said. "I would like a room with a bath."

The class laughed. The coed held her fist up in a victory sign. While Dee flipped to the back of his book, trying to locate the French word for bath. No luck. All he could do was try to hear the next question.

"She wants a room with a bath" the instructor said to the class, holding his book in the air and pointing to a young man on the second row. "So now, how does she ask what it costs per night?"

"Cuanto cuesta por noche?" the young man answered.

"Bueno" said the instructor. "Now, how does she ask where the beauty salon is?"

"Donde està. . ." someone tried to answer. "Wait . . . a beauty salon. . ."

"Donde està el salon de belleza?" answered someone else. Dee could not see who it was. He was busy thumbing through his book. After a moment he got up, walked around his table, and whispered in the ear of the coed with red hair.

"What page are you on?" he asked.

"Chapter two, page forty four" she answered. "You should speak in Spanish when you ask such a stupid question." As she spoke she held her book up so he could see what page she was on.

Dee looked at her book. Green. The same color as the book the instructor was holding. All the books in the room were green. Except his was blue. Green books. A Spanish class. And the clock above the chalkboard said eight thirty.

"Who are you?" the red haired coed asked, turning around and looking at him. "You're not in this class, what are you doing here?"

"Passing through" Dee answered. "On my way to Paris."

"Paris? You look too dumb to go to Paris."

"That's Paris, Texas, lady. Where they all speak English, I hope."

He slipped out the back door of the classroom. Drowsy, heading for the Student Union a block away. When he got there he walked past the coffee shop and up the stairs to a lounge, looking around.

This early in the morning, with no one there, with no one watching television yet, fine. He found a sofa in a corner and stretched out. Heaven, what it must be like to be in heaven. Sound asleep right away.

Only to be awakened again, in the middle of a dream about some place where no one spoke at all, mute and using sign language only. Awakened this time by a single voice. Female, nagging, sounding bossy.

"Wake up" she said. "This is not a flop house."

He sat up and rubbed his eyes.. The coed with red hair. Sitting in an easy chair next to the sofa. With a glass of iced tea in one hand and a book in the other. Staring at him. Disgusted.

"It's you again" she said. "Don't you have some better place to sleep?"

Dee looked at her more closely. Dressed like a model. Silver bracelet, turquoise necklace, diamond earrings, with a frown on her face that said I'm a princess, you're a mile beneath me in the social scale.

"A better place, sure" said Dee. "Your place, let's go there."

"With you? I wouldn't let you near me."

"You said it yourself in class, remember?"

"Really? What did I say?"

"You said my house is your house."

"You're a fool. You should get a job, so you can have a place of your own."

"I have a job, miss. I work for the paper."

"You deliver papers? Perfect, for a tramp like you."

Dee glanced at his watch as she got up to leave. Almost noon, time to catch a bus downtown and meet his folks for lunch. No doubt much to talk about. What's going on at home in Galveston. Why they're headed for Lubbock. Maybe his French class, even.

But sure as hell not about this red haired coed with all her jewels. He watched as she pranced away. "Snotty bitch" he muttered. "One of Hattie's girls could give her a lesson or two in social manners."

"Sit down, I'll order you a bowl of soup" said his mother when he joined his parents in a diner near the paper. Forty years old and still a handsome woman. And still fretting about a son who's almost twenty.

"You look tired" she added. "You're not eating right."

"Damn it Velma, he looks fine" said his father, standing up to greet him.

"Cecil, he does not look fine" said his mother.

"How are you doing, son?" asked his father. "I read your story in the paper."

"From yesterday" said his mother. "It was on the table when we got here."

"A front page byline, that's something" said his father.

"That paper you work for is obscene" said his mother.

"She read the weather page, son. So Alice got six inches, did she?"

"Obscene" his mother said. "Obscene filth."

"So how's college going" asked his father.

"Okay, I guess" said Dee as he sat down, looking at his father. More gray hair now, the same old smile on that wrinkled face. College? No college for him. Not even high school. He's made it on his own. Even if he never talks about it.

"The potato soup, three orders of that" said his mother to the waitress.

"Lubbock, you're on your way out there, what for?" asked Dee.

"Television towers" said his mother. "Tell him, Cecil."

"A whole string of towers, all over West Texas" said his father.

"No more bomb shelters?" asked Dee. "The last I heard you. . ."

"TV towers" said his mother. "That's what his company has him building now."

"Television" said his father. "You ever watch that crap, son? She does."

"Mom, you have a TV set?" asked Dee. "You bought a. . ."

"It's not the Great Depression any more" she said. "We can buy things now."

Dee looked down at his soup as the waitress set a bowl in front of him. Potato soup. A feast when you're poor, and little, and always hungry. And now they have a TV set? She's right. It's not the Great Depression any more. No more going hungry. No more eating potato soup, no more. . .

"Everybody's buying things" said his father. "We're getting spoiled."

"Not spoiled" said his mother. "We're just getting over the Depression."

"Spoiled and soft" said his father. "After the war, get everything you can."

"Things we never had before" said his mother. "It's not about the war, Cecil."

"Velma, it's the war that got us out of the Depression" said his father.

"Not the war" said his mother. "It was President Roosevelt."

"It was the war" said his father. "Roosevelt wasn't God, he couldn't do it."

"Cecil, you don't know about God" said his mother. "You never go to church."

"No" said his father. "But I built one up near Waco, that was enough."

Dee looked down at the soup and pushed it away. Listening, more or less. The usual back and forth, his father never letting up, building things for the war, getting them out of the poor house, always going at it with her about religion, about the Baptists, about the way she. . .

"Phil, that Bible I gave you" said his mother, "do you ever read it?"

"I know what it says" Dee answered. "I've read it, every word of it."

"It's best to be a Christian" she said. "It gives you something to believe in."

"Like that nitwit sister of mine" said his father. "Look at her."

"Cecil, you shouldn't talk about Mabel Jean that way" said his mother.

"Really?" he replied. "You remember that summer she beat the hell out of Phil?"

Dee glanced at his father and nodded. Mabel Jean, right, whipping him with a tree branch, when he was ten years old, staying with her in East Texas. Screaming God would send him to hell for playing with the nigger kids from across the railroad tracks.

"Mabel Jean has changed" said his mother. "She cares about Phil."

"Like hell she does" said his father. "What makes you think she cares?"

"Because she asked me" said his mother. "Why he has to work to go to school."

"He doesn't have to" said his father. "He has a damned good job, that's all."

"She asked me why we don't pay for him go to school" said his mother.

"He's not spoiled, that's why" said his father. "He wants to do it on his own. And he can write, Velma, remember? He showed that in high school."

"But see how sleepy he is" said his mother. "He's so tired he's let us do all the talking." She stared at Dee, shaking her head.

He was sleepy, all right. With his mind now on something he hadn't thought about lately. Getting the hell away from all the Mabel Jeans in the world, away from East Texas.

"Son, you're doing fine" said his father. "But we have to go, we're running late."

"It's a long way to Lubbock" said his mother. "You take care, Phil."

Dee followed them out of the diner, told them he would see them at Thanksgiving when they got back, and hugged them both goodbye. Spoiled? No way. Another year at the University, keep Buck from firing him, get away from East Texas for good.

Dee walked from the diner to the downtown police station, met the desk sergeant, told him he was new on the police beat, and he could use all the help he could get. The sergeant showed him the daily record book and how to read it. We call it the blotter he said. Dee made some notes, thanked him, and headed for work.

When he entered the newspaper office he stopped, straightened his tie, went to his desk, and started typing. Then he got up and handed his copy to the city editor. Amos Ashley, middle aged, gray haired, his feet propped on his desk, indifferent to the cigar smoke and all the noise, phones ringing, teletypes clattering, people yelling.

"First day on the police beat" said Ashley, reading what Dee had written. "Looks like you've had a good start at the station."

"So far, two robberies, a cat stuck in a sewer pipe, that's all" said Dee.

"The police save a cat. Good. Human interest, two paragraphs, that's enough."

"Okay, but don't let Lulu write the headline, Amos."

"I know. I can see it now. Cops love a little pussy. That woman's a pain in the ass, look at her, dumb as hell, sitting there acting innocent."

Dee turned toward the ring, a circular table where Lulu sat between two men, all three writing headlines on stories shoved to them by the makeup editor. An old man, maybe too tired sometimes to catch Lulu's latest double-entendre. A French word, he'd seen it in his book. Innocent, hell.

"You think she's dumb, Amos? I think she knows what she's up to."

"Damn it, I can't fire her, Buck won't let me, she's one of his pets."

"I know" said Dee. She was in the Navy. I wonder what she looked like in a uniform." Dee watched as Lulu got up from the ring, took her purse and started down the hall, no doubt headed for the ladies' room. Thirty or so, not bad looking at all, reminding him of one of Hattie's girls.

"To hell with her" said Amos. "Listen, I want you to get out of the station."

"What? What was that?"

"Start riding in a police car. That's how you get to know them."

"Get to know who?"

"The police, damn it, pay attention."

Dee turned back to Ashley as Lulu disappeared down the hallway. "All right" he said. "I'll ride around in a police car. That sounds more exciting."

"Excitement, hell, you want excitement, go see Buck, he's waiting for you."

"Buck? He wants to see me again? What for?"

"I don't know. Some crap about the mayor, I think."

"The mayor? He's not part of the police beat, he's. . ."

"Go see him, your buddies are there already."

Ashley went back to marking copy, but he held a hand up so Dee would not walk away. "I almost forgot, Phil. Here's something that is on your beat. A man named Trembley, the oldest retired cop in Austin. He called in, here's his number. See him, write a feature story on him. Now go see Buck and your pals."

They were standing in front of Buck's desk, Galloway and Parker, all three of them yelling, so loud Dee could hear them in the hall before he got there. The yelling stopped when Buck saw him coming. Parker opened the door to Buck's office, smiling, almost grinning, and Dee entered.

He looked around. All quiet now. No one speaking. Galloway with his arms crossed, wearing his broken straw hat, Parker in his rumpled linen suit, with the sleeve sewn up, Buck at his desk, looking down at a note, while Dee waited to hear what new trouble he had stumbled into.

"All right, Phil" said Buck. "Where were you at three this morning?"

"At home, trying to study French" Dee answered. "What's this about?"

"This note" said Buck. "The mayor, raising hell about your two pals here."

"The mayor's full of shit" said Galloway. "I told you, he's lying."

"Maybe he is" said Buck, speaking louder. "But he's still the goddamn mayor." He got up, came around his desk, and poked his finger in Galloway's chest, starting to yell again, with Galloway yelling back. Dee sat down in a corner chair, leaned back and listened, trying to make some sense of all the shouting.

Buck, yelling at Galloway, telling him again what the note said. How the mayor and an aide had been drinking quietly in a downtown bar at three in the morning. How Galloway had come in with Parker and grabbed the mayor's cap. All because the cap was maroon and white, from Texas A & M.

Galloway, yelling back, telling Buck that's bullshit, there's no downtown bar open at three in the morning, the only place open that late is Hattie's, the mayor was drunk and bragging how the Aggies would whip the Longhorns this time around, and when he'd said kiss off the mayor had grabbed his straw had and stepped on it.

Parker, joining in, shouting Jack's right, Little Bob stomped on his hat, and his fucking aide, look what he did, he ripped the sleeve off my suit when I reached down for the hat, I'll have to have a new suit when I judge that cheerleader contest next week, that's fifty dollars, ask the mayor who's going to pay for that.

Buck leaned against his desk as the shouting died down. "I'll call Hattie" he said, speaking softly. "Maybe she can tell me what happened." He reached for the mayor's note, threw it in a waste basket, and looked at Dee, sitting in the corner.

"Phil, how old are you?" he asked.

"Nineteen" Dee answered. "Twenty in October."

"Jack, you and Steve, how old are you?"

"Twenty six" said Galloway. "Do that, call Hattie."

"The same" said Parker. "Call the mayor, too, ask him about a new suit."

"Nineteen, twenty six, twenty six" said Buck. "Too bad you weren't in the war. When are you going to grow up?"

"Your war" said Parker. "Damn it, Buck, Jack and I were both in Korea."

"Korea, hell" said Buck. "Get out of my damn office."

At two in the morning a patrol car stopped on Loraine Street. The policeman driving the car switched off the lights. Turning his head to look in the back seat at Dee, asking a question. "Fourteen oh one Loraine, that's your address, kid?"

"Correct" said Dee. "Thanks for the ride. Interesting evening."

"We've been here before" said the other policeman. Not as tall as the driver, sitting on the right side of the front seat. "Two or three times, complaints about noise."

"Really" said Dee. "Complaints. I'll be damned."

"Complaints" said the driver. "Not like that broad at the grocery tonight."

"Right" said the other policeman. "A five pound ham in her brassiere, kid, and all she did was laugh about it. Good looking chippy, too bad we had to book her."

"Something to write about" said Dee. "You want to come in for a drink?"

"Nope" said the driver. "That broad, she'll be getting out on bail pretty soon."

"With plenty of ham for us both" said the other policeman. "Take care, kid."

Dee said thanks and got out of the car, watching as they disappeared around a corner. Heading back to the station, it looked like. "Something to write about, indeed" he mumbled. "Two horny cops, a load of ham, and a chippy to do the roasting."

He walked past the buildings on the street, along a gravel driveway to a courtyard in the rear, and stood for a moment under a tree, looking up at a second floor apartment. The only one with lights on. Quiet. No complaints tonight.

Quiet, even as a black Mercedes drove into the courtyard. In the moonlight Dee could see the driver getting out of the car. Buck, carrying a package. Going up the outside stairs to the apartment with the lights on.

"Buck, what's he doing here?" Dee muttered. "Damn it, I've had enough of his biting my ass." He leaned against the tree, waiting for Buck to leave. No sign of that. After a few minutes he went up the stairs, holding his breath.

When he entered the apartment Buck was standing at the bar next to Parker, with Galloway behind it. "Phil, old buddy, you're here, have a drink" said Galloway when he saw him. "Look at my new hat the boss delivered."

"Straw, like your old one" said Buck. "Hattie sent it, I told you. So this is where you idiots hang out. Loraine Street."

"Three months now" said Parker. "Nice, except for the neighbors."

"So I've heard" said Buck. "This bar, where in hell did you get it?"

"It's a loan from Herman" said Parker. "Hattie, that's all she sent?"

"A hat for Jack, with a note saying tell the mayor to kiss her ass."

"Here's to the mayor" said Galloway. "You need a drink, boss."

"Not out of this glass" said Buck. "It has lipstick on it."

Dee sat down as Buck looked around, saw the kitchen, and went searching for another glass. Sounds from the kitchen then. Cabinet doors being slammed, Buck groaning, water running. When he came back he was wiping a glass with a paper towel.

"Three months" he said. "This place looks like a ship wreck."

"Can't hire a maid" said Parker. "We're broke."

"Where we work, they pay us slave wages" said Galloway.

"Slave wages, my ass" said Buck. "That trash barrel in your kitchen, there must be fifty empty liquor bottles in it."

"They're for Herman" said Parker. "He refills them. Discount service."

"Herman, no shit" said Buck. "Pour me some Scotch, Jack, straight, no ice."

As Galloway reached for a bottle under the bar Buck turned to Parker, looking at his suit with the sleeve sewn back. "All right, Steve" he said. "What's this crap you told me in my office, something about a beauty contest you're judging."

"Not a beauty context, Buck. A cheerleader tryout."

"So you need a new suit. The mayor's aide tore this one, you said."

"At Hattie's, when I reached down, when I tried to save Jack's hat."

"In the Nay, we'd call that line of duty. You know what that means?"

"What? A medal? I'm supposed to settle for that?"

"It means we'd pay for it out of a slush fund. How much did it cost?"

"Three hundred dollars. It's Bombay linen."

"Bombay, my ass. El Paso. Twenty dollars on Congress Street."

Buck drank from the glass Galloway handed him and smiled at Parker. The master of a ship now, in charge of the crew. He finished the Scotch in three or four swallows and ordered another one. Looking around the room. Seeing Dee in the corner.

"Phil, why are you up so late?" he wanted to know.

"I've been riding around with cops" Dee answered.

"Damn it, why did I put you on the police beat? Remember?"

"So I could get some sleep, you said, but I. . ."

"So you could finish school and get out of my hair."

"Look, Buck, I'm trying, I'm taking a course this summer, I. . ."

"One course, that's all? What time does it meet?"

"Early . . . seven in the morning . . . a French class. . ."

"Seven. From now on, you get back by ten at night, you hear? Right now, go hit the sack. No more riding around with cops this late. Understand?"

Dee got up, shrugged his shoulders, and headed for his bedroom. Orders. First that crap about D-Day and the sailors, and now Buck was treating him like some kind of swabbie, or whatever they called them in the Navy.

"Cops" said Buck as Dee went off to bed. "The shore patrol. I've heard they've been here."

"Shore patrol, no way" said Parker.

"Cops" said Buck. "Word gets around. How many times have they been here?"

"Cops? You see any cops?" Parker asked Galloway.

"No cops" said Galloway. "You must have the wrong address, Buck."

Buck emptied his glass and shook his head. Looking at Galloway and Parker, face to face. He started laughing then. Looking around the room. Back at the kitchen. At Herman's bar.

"What's so funny?" asked Parker.

"You two" said Buck. "You remind me of a couple of sailors I knew."

"The Navy" said Galloway. "Two sailors, what about them?"

"Total fuck ups" said Buck.

"Not like us at all" said Parker. "So what?"

"They fell overboard. The sharks got them."

"That's nothing to laugh about" said Galloway. "You need another drink."

"More Scotch, keep pouring. I'm telling you, watch out."

"For what?" asked Parker.

"For the shore patrol and the sharks, that's what" said Buck. "Right now, drink up, you two, it's anchors aweigh. Here's to the Navy."

Three nights later Dee looked at his watch as he came out of his room with a can of beer in one hand and his French book in the other. Not quite ten thirty in the evening. Way too early for the noise he heard. Way too early for the bar to be open.

But open it was. With Parker behind it, in his new linen suit, waving his arms, like an orchestra conductor. And in the middle of the room, two young women in flimsy costumes, orange and white, jumping up and down and yelling.

"Texas fight!" they shouted, keeping pace with the sound of the Longhorn marching band, coming from the record player near the bar. "Texas fight! And it's goodbye to A and M. Texas fight! Texas fight! And we'll put over one more win."

"Okay, ladies, that's a start" said Parker as he turned the music down. "You get a drink now." They rushed to the bar. Parker dropped some ice cubes in two glasses, poured in liquor, and handed them a reward.

Dee looked. Clean glasses, a half dozen on the bar. Clean glasses? Where did they come from? These two women, with their hair dyed orange, where did they come from? Parker, giving them drinks, what in hell was he up to?

Not just these two women. Two more in the kitchen. Dee walked by them, to the trash barrel to toss away his beer can. And saw what they were doing. The dishes. Both of them dressed in orange and white, up to their elbows in soapsuds.

"This will take all night" said the one on the left. A bit pudgy around the waist, Dee noticed. "Let's dry this pile I've washed" said the other one, not so pudgy, downright skinny. Both of them with the same orange hair.

The pudgy one opened a drawer filled with dishtowels never used. She turned around when she heard Dee drop his empty beer can in the barrel. "Who are you?" she asked. "What are you doing here?"

"A neighbor" he answered. "Just passing through on my way to Paris" he added, holding up his French book.

"You're from France?" she giggled "You know how to French kiss?"

"Sure, in the ear" said Dee.

"Don't look in there" she said as he opened the refrigerator. "It's full of goo."

"And beer" he replied, reaching for another can.

"That's one more thing we have to do" said the skinny one without looking up. "Clean the refrigerator."

"Anything for a drink" said the pudgy one, smiling at Dee.

"Steve, that's what he promised us, a drink" said the skinny one.

"Steve? Who's that?" asked Dee.

"He lives here" she answered. "He was one of our judges tonight."

"The cheerleader contest" said the skinny one. "They didn't pick us."

"Applause" said the pudgy one. "We didn't get enough applause. Steve said he called the paper with a story about us, he said he'd put in a good word."

As she spoke she reached for the can Dee had opened, took a sip, and smiled. When she gave it back he saw a birthmark near her right hand. And remembered what someone told him when he was growing up in East Texas.

Beware of girls with birthmarks on their hands.

Nothing to beware of right then. Except for police. With Parker at the bar, turning the music back to loud, sounding drunk as he yelled to the kitchen, saying hurry up, it's curtain call.

Dee looked at his watch and figured ten minutes at most. With all this noise someone will call them. Ten minutes and the police will be here.

The two in the kitchen wiped soapsuds from their cheerleader costumes, threw the towels on the counter, and joined the others in front of the bar. Parker lined them up as Dee watched. Four abreast, so to speak, ready to show some team spirit.

"Texas fight! Texas fight! And it's goodbye to A and M" they started yelling, kicking their legs in the air. Until Parker turned the music down, came around the bar, and stopped them. Telling them to work on it, kick their legs up higher.

"It's too warm in here for these" said the pudgy one, grabbing at her hair. She pulled off a wig. Orange, blonde underneath it, Dee noticed. The others did the same. They took off their wigs and stacked them on the bar.

"It's too warm for almost anything" said the skinny one. "Unless you give us something nice and cold to drink." Parker nodded, dropped ice cubes in four glasses, and poured more liquor.

They gulped the drinks. Giggling and burping. Parker stuck one of the orange wigs sideways on his head, staggered around the bar, lined them up and mumbled "Here, I'll show you how to do it."

They stood side by side then, the way he told them. With their arms on each other's shoulders, kicking their legs up, first their left legs, then their right legs, more or less together, like the cancan dancers Dee had seen in a movie about Paris.

Parker turned on the music and they went at it again, kicking their legs in the air. "Texas fight! Texas fight! And it's goodbye to A and M. Texas fight! Texas fight! And we'll put over one more win."

As loud as they could. Until the skinny one slipped and fell on the floor. Bringing the others down with her. All four, sprawled on the floor, laughing, unable to get up with their legs tangled together.

Parker turned off the music and staggered away from the bar. Standing over them, looking down as they tried to stand up. "Well, hell" he said. "Go finish up in the kitchen, we'll give it another try when you're done."

Quiet, then, as the four got to their feet and stumbled off to the kitchen. Washing and drying dishes. Cleaning the counter. Three of them at that, while the skinny one cleaned out the refrigerator.

Quiet. Until the police showed up and knocked on the door.

Dee recognized them when he let them in. The tall one, the short one with him, the two who busted the chippy with the ham in her brassiere. Bored, it looked like, in about the same mood as last time.

"The reporter from the paper" said the tall one. "You live here, kid?" Dee nodded, noticing the policeman's nameplate. Bordon.

"What's this, high drag?" asked the other one when he saw the orange wig on Parker's head. Jody, his nameplate said. Parker took the wig off and stayed silent.

"Your neighbors" said the tall one, Bordon. "They've been complaining again, about the noise from this apartment."

"Noise?" Parker replied, leaning against the bar. "Noise? It's quiet, I don't hear any noise."

"Who's that in the kitchen?" asked the tall one, Bordon, looking around. "Those broads in there, who are they?"

"Maids" said Parker. "Doing the dishes. They must have dropped one, if somebody heard some noise."

"Nice looking maids" said the short policeman, Jody. "I'll bring them out for questioning."

Just as Dee expected. Four would-be cheerleaders, drunk, at the mercy of two policemen who specialized in late night social work. No doubt ready to check their brassieres for shoplifted ham, or whatever else they could get their hands on.

"Underage drinking" said Bordon, looking back and forth at the evidence. Empty glasses on the bar, four young women with their hands in the air, giggling as they came marching from the kitchen. With his comrade Officer Jody behind them. Grinning.

"How old are you?" asked Bordon. The women looked at each other, uncertain what to say. Except for the pudgy one.

"Thirty five" she said. "Going on forty."

"Show me some ID" said the short policeman, Jody. "Your driver's license."

"In my pants" she said. "You want to feel and see?"

"Don't touch me" said the skinny one. "Look in my purse over there."

Officer Jody brought their purses from the corner where they had piled them. "Which one belongs to you?" he asked the pudgy girl.

"The red one" she laughed. "Watch out, there's a loaded pistol in there."

"Nothing but some lipstick and a license" said Jody. "You're nineteen."

"Jail bait" said Bordon.

"Maybe, maybe not" said Jody. "You young ladies, go get in that patrol car downstairs. No more washing dishes tonight, you hear?"

Dee watched as Officer Jody led them down the stairs. Stumbling and giggling. No more kitchen work tonight, indeed. Maybe their cheerleader show for the cops instead. Show them how high they kick their legs in the air.

"Next time, hire some maids a little older" Bordon said to Parker.

"We'll do that" he answered. "You want a drink?"

"Nope. We've got some work to do. Keep it quiet now, Steve."

When they were gone Dee went to the kitchen and stood back, marveling at how clean things were. He opened another can of beer and started to his bedroom to study. With his French book in his hand. One hell of a night, he grumbled. Then he stopped, turned around and looked at Parker, leaning against the bar.

"Damn it, Steve, you could have gotten us both arrested."

"No way" he answered. "That cop, Bordon, we were in the Army together."

At three in the afternoon, when Dee arrived for work, the same old story.

Ashley, with his feet propped on his desk, with a grease pencil in his hand, marking the paper page by page, as usual not looking up, saying Buck's waiting for you, go see him.

"What is it this time?" asked Dee.

"Some friends he wants you to meet. You'll find them charming."

"Charming? I'll bet. Amos, listen, when I get back, we need to talk."

Ashley replied "No doubt" and marked another story. Dee walked to Buck's office, wondering what that meant. No doubt? No doubt about what?

A couple, middle aged, Dee noticed as he entered the office. Buck made the introductions. Andrew and Deloris something or other, with Andrew looking at the pictures on the wall, while the woman sat in the corner, holding the morning paper in her lap, going through the classified pages, the apartment ads, it looked like.

"Andy was on my ship" said Buck. "We haven't seen each other in years."

"Right" said Andrew. "When we heard about Buck, we came in to see him."

"You heard about him?" asked Dee. "What? I'd like to hear myself."

"Sit down, Andy" said Buck. "You too, Phil."

"I will, I'm tired" said Andrew. "Buck tells us you're one of his reporters."

"Working my way through college" said Dee. "With guidance from him."

"My husband's a pharmacist" said the woman. "We just moved here."

"Great" said Dee. "Maybe he can give me some pills to stay awake."

"Phil doesn't get much sleep" said Buck. "He's on the police beat."

The woman looked at Dee for a moment, nodding. She turned to her husband then and whispered something. A question, not loud enough for Dee to hear. No trouble hearing Andrew's answer. Go ahead and ask him, Deloris, he's on the police beat, if Buck doesn't know what we can do about the cops, maybe he will.

"The police" she said. "We've had some trouble with them."

"I'm sorry" Dee replied. "I can't get them to fix any parking tickets."

"No, it's where we live" she said. "They won't do anything about the noise."

"It's noise upstairs" said Andrew. We've called the cops a dozen times."

"It's always the same" said Deloris. "We complain, they say call the owner."

"But the owner lives in Dallas" said Andrew. "We can't even reach him."

"It's weird" said Deloris. "It's quiet, then it starts about two in the morning."

"Last night, a little earlier" said Andrew. "A pep rally, it sounded like."

"My, my" said Buck. "Deloris, where did you say you live?"

"Loraine Street" she answered. "Fourteen oh one Loraine."

Dee looked at Buck. Who was smiling. And telling his friends he doubted Phil could do much about it, since he was only a reporter working his way through college, but he knew that neighborhood, he would see what he could do about the noise himself.

"Please do" said Deloris, starting to get up. "We have to go."

"Phil, here's my card" said Andrew. "Come by, I'll give you something."

"To keep you awake" said Deloris. "What we need is the opposite."

"Until we can move" said Andrew. "We're looking around right now."

Dee stood up, acting polite as they got up to leave. Hearing Andrew tell Buck he would see him later, watching him take his wife's arm, both of them going through the apartment ads as they left the office. He looked down at Buck then, sitting at his desk, leaning back and grinning.

"That was chicken shit, Buck. Setting me up like that."

"Damned right. Watch out for sharks and the shore patrol."

"That couple, what about them? You treated them like puppets."

"Hell, Andy's in business now, the way you idiots behave, I need all the damned pills he can feed me."

Pills, fine. No mention of what Buck had in mind when he told them he knew their neighborhood, he would check around himself about the noise. Whatever it was, Ashley must have known, the way he sounded when Dee got back to his desk.

"Nice couple" said Ashley. "After tonight, their troubles are over."

"Tonight? What happens tonight?"

"Buck grilled your buddy Parker. He called the police chief then."

"The police chief? Where's Parker? What did he say?"

"Ask him yourself, he's down at the Paramount, covering a movie."

"Ask him what? What's going on here, Amos?"

"You can't figure it out? You must be dumber than I thought."

Dumb. Or worse, perhaps. Trying to remember what he had meant to ask when he first arrived, when Ashley said "No doubt." Looking at the envelope Ashley handed him without looking up. Opening the envelope and reading the note inside, wondering what that meant.

A message from Galloway. Short, hand written, in Galloway's standard scribble. Be at the apartment tonight at 11:00, I will pick you up and show you something you can write about for the police beat.

Dee looked at the note and remembered. The police, that's what he had wanted to ask about. Who decides the route they follow. No way to ask right now, not with Ashley up and headed down the hall to see Buck in his office.

No doubt? Dee nodded. Whatever Galloway had in mind, that was something else, but what Ashley meant by "No doubt" was starting to sink in.

"Drop me off at the Tavern" said Dee as the patrol car turned onto Tenth Street. "I'll have a beer and walk home from there."

"Twelfth and Lamar, you're on, kid" said Bordon. "Grab that French book you carry around, hell yes, we'll have one with you."

"Might as well" said the policeman in the right seat, the short one, Jody. Laughing. "Our last night around here, no more roasted ham for us."

"They've changed your route?" asked Dee. "Imagine that."

"South of the river now" said the driver. "At least it's not East Austin."

"Nigger town" said the other policeman. "Nothing out there but spare ribs."

Bordon pulled into the parking lot behind the Tavern, turned off the engine, and wrote something on a clipboard. "Car trouble, a half hour to fix a flat" he said to the other policeman, Jody, and got out of the car.

In the parking lot, in the bright lights behind the Tavern, Dee saw something he had not noticed when they picked him up at the station. Their faces. Both of them, their faces covered with scratches.

And then something else, as he followed them through the door. How they looked at the tables filled with people drinking beer, stopped, turned around and left, back to the patrol car in the parking lot. Gone, not saying a word.

Odd, even for them. Dee watched through a window as they drove away. He went to the bar then, put his French book down, and ordered a stein of Lone Star draft. Looking up at a bear hide on the wall, six feet long, with a clock mounted in the middle. Nine fifty, plenty of time for a beer.

The bartender pushed the beer to Dee, but it was out of reach before he could touch it. He looked down and saw where the stein had gone. In the hand with a birthmark above it. The pudgy blonde, standing behind him and laughing.

"What are you doing in here?" he asked. "You're underage."

"Fake IDs" she whispered in his ear. "Come and join us."

He had to. She was holding his beer. And was leading him to a table in the corner, where the rest of her cheerleader team was sitting. Two brunettes and the skinny girl. In different costumes now, all four wearing polka dot dresses, the skinny one giving him a hard look as he sat down.

"Those two pricks you came in with" she said. "You hang around with them?"

"Not any more" said Dee. "Not where they'll be working from now on."

"Working?" she replied. "You'd call that working, what they tried with us?"

"No, damn it, you'd call it rape" said one of the brunettes.

"That night they dragged us out of your apartment" said the other brunette.

"It's Steve's fault, for taking us there in the first place" said the skinny one.

"This too, this is his fault" said the first brunette, reaching in her purse for a newspaper clipping. Dee looked at it and smiled. Lulu's headline on a three-paragraph story about cheerleaders being chosen by applause, the story Parker called in:

UT GIRLS
GET CLAPS

"Claps" she grumbled. "We don't have any filthy claps."

"That's what you get when you sit on dirty toilet seats" said the skinny one.

"No, it's what you get from cops" said the first brunette.

"I'd like to rip their balls off" said the first brunette. "Real assholes."

"Cowards, too" said the skinny one. "You saw how they ran when they saw us."

"So what do you want me to do?" asked Dee. "Apologize for them?"

"No" said the pudgy blonde. "We want you to drink your beer and be nice."

She handed him his stein and reached down, patting Dee's leg and smiling. While the others went on yakking. About the two policemen. How they fought them off, starting to laugh about it. How, according to the first brunette, she had kicked the short cop in the you-know-what and sent him off screaming.

"What's your name?" the pudgy blonde asked Dee.

"Omar Khayyam" he answered. "What's yours?"

"Debbie Decker" she said. " Omar? That's not French."

"It is, too" said the skinny girl. "It's the name of a French pirate."

"A famous one" said the first brunette. "He sailed in the Caribbean Ocean."

"No" said the other one. "He was a trader, he sold jewels to the Indians."

"Right" said the first brunette. "I remember now, I saw a movie about him."

"A French trader" said the other one. "They named the O.K. Corral for him."

"My grandfather" said Dee. "I'm following in his footsteps."

"Really?" Debbie laughed, rubbing his leg. "What are you trading?"

Dee tried to push her away, looking at the clock on the bear hide. It's getting late, I've got to get home, he told them, you ladies guessed right, I have to study French if I'm going to make it back to my granddad's place in Paris.

"We'll give you a ride" said the skinny girl, looking at Debbie and smiling.

"We have a car in the parking lot" said Debbie. "You can't walk home like that."

Dee stood up and followed them out of the Tavern. Holding his book down low, with the pages open, trying to hide his you-know-what. Stiff. Embarrassed. Almost groaning. Really groaning when he saw what he'd have to ride home in.

An old Ford coupe, with a rumble seat in the back, the rear window open, and the skinny girl getting ready to drive. He tried to get in the front seat beside her, but one of the brunettes beat him to it, laughing, saying no, sit in the back with Debbie.

He climbed in the rumble seat, with Debbie on his lap, the other brunette squeezed in beside them, the car shaking and rattling as the skinny girl started the engine, smoke coming from the exhaust pipe, Dee holding his book, Debbie rubbing and Dee moaning.

"You're going the wrong way" he yelled through the window.

"The long way around" the skinny girl yelled back. "Right, Debbie?"

"You bet" she yelled back. "Omar needs a few more minutes."

The long way around then, along Lamar, the car bouncing up and down as the skinny girl turned on to a side street. When they finally stopped at his apartment, Debbie stood up so he could climb out. He did, holding his book up so she could see it.

"Omar, you look out of breath" said Debbie.

"I am" said Dee. "I've never studied so hard."

They drove off. Laughing, all four. Debbie, standing up in the rumble seat, looking back at Dee. Yelling I'll see you around the campus, Omar. And remember, Texas Fight! Texas Fight!

Dee went upstairs, took a shower, and changed his underwear. Waiting for Galloway to pick him up. Smiling. Remembering that warning from East Texas. Beware of girls with birthmarks on their hands.

REBELS

"I could be wrong" said Galloway as he drove down the hill. "It may be false alarm, but if it's not it should make a helluva story."

"This late at night, Steve, let's hope it's worth it" said Dee. "For the police beat, you said, what kind of story?"

"Trespassing, statutory rape" said Galloway, chewing on an unlit cigar. "Plus running around nude in public, how's that?"

"Maybe, maybe not, a couple of paragraphs at most. Not much of a crime, and anyway, why are you laughing?"

"A bet I heard about. You'll see" said Galloway as he turned off Lamar on to Twenty Fourth Street, heading to the University.

When he crossed Guadalupe he turned on a side street and parked in front of the football stadium. Quiet, no one around. "Here, take these binoculars" said Galloway. "If I'm right, you'll need them."

Dee followed him to the gate. Where a man was waiting. Big, heavy set, wearing a Texas jacket and a Longhorn cap, it looked like, but even in the moonlight it was far too dark to see his face.

"Wilbur, this is Phillip Dee" said Galloway. "He's with me."

"Dee, sure, I've read your stuff in the paper" said Wilbur.

"He covers police" said Galloway.

"Not that" said Wilbur. "That D-day story, you quoted my nephew Arnie."

"Arnie, right" said Dee. "The night jump he made in Normandy, quite a story."

"Paratroopers, all a bit crazy" said Wilbur. "Arnie, too, the way he jokes around. Let's go in, we're about ready."

"Wilbur's the athletic director" said Galloway. "He's going to show us the new lights, Phil."

"New candlepower" said Wilbur. "So Jack can write about it in his column."

Dee followed them under the stadium, then up a ramp to some seats in the middle. Wondering. Why Galloway had dragged him here in the middle of the night. Why he mentioned a bet he heard about. Why he handed him binoculars. What stadium lights might have to do with the police beat.

"Here we go" said Wilbur as he flipped a switch and turned the lights on.

Bright. Blinding, for a few seconds. Then, when his eyes cleared, Dee saw something odd through the binoculars.

More than odd. On the fifty yard line, a blanket, with clothes nearby. A woman running around in circles, nude, screaming, looking up at the lights, rubbing her eyes, trying to find something to put on, disappearing naked under the stadium.

And standing on the blanket, also nude, a man. Calm, bending over, finding his trousers, reaching in the pocket and bringing out a pack of cigarettes. Lighting one and looking up at the sky, as if nothing had happened.

Wilbur grabbed the binoculars from Dee. "Goddamn" he yelled. "That's Arnie, what's he doing?"

Winning a bet, maybe, Dee started to answer. But said nothing.

"Get your clothes on, go home" yelled Wilbur as loud as he could.

Arnie heard his voice, looked up, and saluted. Just as Wilbur turned the lights off. Dark again, pitch black. When he could see well enough Wilbur handed back the binoculars, silent, and led them down the ramp, underneath the stadium.

"Jack, do me a favor" he said when they reached the gate. "Don't write about this."

"How could I?" Galloway answered. "No way, even if that wasn't your nephew."

"Arnie, damn it, he knew about these lights. Somebody put him up to this."

Dee followed Galloway to his car and got in. Smiling. With his mind at work, dreaming up a better twist on what he'd seen. Arnie, naked on the fifty yard line. Debbie Decker and her goofy comrades.

"Sorry" said Galloway. "I thought there would be a story for you."

"I'm thinking of one" said Dee.

"Not now, Wilbur won't press charges against his own damned nephew."

"How did you know about this, Jack? Who told you?"

"Herman. He said there was a big bet going down."

"Arnie. Getting laid on the fifty yard line, hell, he must have won a bundle."

"Ask Herman, he'll know. Just don't try to write about it, Phil."

"No way. Wonder why Herman didn't tell me, too. I could have had some cheerleaders there for Arnie, four of them, yelling Texas Fight!"

"You can ask him yourself" said Galloway. "That's him, coming from the stadium." In the darkness, Dee could see Herman coming from beneath the stands. With another man. Checking to see how the bet had gone, perhaps.

Dee leaned back as Galloway started the engine. Can't write about this, what Arnie just pulled off? With his eyes wide open he could see the headline Lulu would come up with:

Turn Off The Lights
PARATROOPER SCORES
FROM FIFTY YARD LINE

"What are you laughing about" asked Galloway as they drove on.

"Headlines" said Dee. "Too bad I can't write about Arnie."

Someone he could write about, Dee knew as soon as he met him, Trembley, the oldest retired policeman in Austin. The man Ashley told him to interview, after Trembley called the paper. He was old, all right, out of the hospital now and ready to talk, sitting there on the sofa in a small brick home, holding hands with his wife, as old as him. Eighty at least.

"Jason's feeling better" said his wife, "but he's awfully upset."

"I am" said Trembley. "The chief wouldn't listen when I warned him."

"Warned him about what?" asked Dee, opening his note pad.

"There's something crooked going on" said Trembley. "Tell him, Martha."

"In East Austin" said his wife. "Where the black folks live."

"The chief, I don't like to go behind his back" said Trembley. "But. . ."

"I'm all ears" Dee interrupted. "Let's get this picture first."

They sat up straight while the photographer with Dee focused his Speed Graphic and took two pictures, with flashbulbs, the old couple blinking and rubbing their eyes after he had finished and left.

"Too bright" said his wife. "Not like the old days."

"They used something else back then, like gun powder" said Trembley.

"That picture up there, that was with that kind of powder" said his wife.

"That's us when we got married" said Trembley.

"Fifty five years ago this Christmas" said his wife.

"You can take it with you" said Trembley. "Use it in the paper if you promise to bring it back." Dee stood up and looked at the pictures on the wall. Turning brown, but still sharp enough to print. Yes, he said, this one too, with you in uniform, back in the twenties, I would guess, that will go well with what I'm going to write.

"The one next to it, that little girl, that's Martha" said Trembley.

"On our farm out west" she added. "Before the Comanches burned us out."

"They killed half her family" said Trembley. "The rest moved here."

"To Austin" she said. "When I grew up that's how I met Jason."

"When was that?" asked Dee. "I mean, when did they burn you out?"

"That would have been in the seventies" she said. "The eighteen seventies."

"The Comanches" said Trembley, "they almost got to Austin."

"The one who led them, he was a half-breed" said Trembley's wife.

"Really . . . no . . . I didn't know that" Dee replied, writing as fast as he could.

"Quanta Parker" said Trembley. "He finally gave up and surrendered."

"They should have shot him" said his wife, getting up from the sofa.

"No, Martha, you don't shoot someone who's surrendered" said Trembley as she walked away. Still spry for her age, Dee noticed. When she returned with a tray of iced tea and cookies he said thanks and watched as Trembley tried to hold the glass she handed him. Not easy. His hands were shaky. An old man, for sure.

"So what was it like, when you were with the police?" Dee asked.

"A lot of parades" said Trembley. "The Civil War parade was always best."

"Every year" said his wife. "It would always end with the rebel yell."

"The rebel yell, as loud as they could" added Trembley. "They're all gone now."

"Parades" said Dee. "Regular police work, what about that?"

Trembley sipped from his glass of iced tea, looking up at the pictures on the wall, then across the room at some medals and trophies liked up on the mantle above the fire place. Deep in thought for a moment or so before he spoke.

"Prohibition" said Trembley. "It was all about Prohibition in the twenties."

"Speakeasies" his wife added. "I went to a few with my girlfriends."

"We left them alone" said Trembley. "It was the bootleggers we were after."

"Ever catch any?" asked Dee, turning the page in his notepad.

"On the road to Temple" said Trembley. "We ambushed truckloads."

"They'd have caught a lot more if they'd gone to East Austin" said his wife.

"We stayed out of East Austin" said Trembley. "All black, we stayed away."

"But not these days" said his wife. "The police don't stay away any more."

Dee glanced up from his notepad and saw they were looking at each other, shaking their heads. Martha whispered something in her husband's ear, he whispered something back, and then he spoke, slowly, shaking his head.

"That's what I tried to tell the chief" he said. "About what's going on now."

"The last few years" said his wife. "It's how they've been voting over there." "The police, it looks like they're involved in rigging votes" said Trembley.

"Rigging votes?" asked Dee, looking up from his notepad.

"Making sure they vote a certain way" said Trembley.

"Our maid, she's the one who first told us about it" said his wife.

"I've checked it out" said Trembley. "It' crooked, what's going on."

"That's why Jason called the paper" said his wife.

"Good . . . you did the right thing" said Dee, writing, and then looking up when Trembley's wife said Jason, you're tired, you need to rest now. She helped him up from the sofa and guided him away, Trembley limping, using a cane, barely able to move. Dee waited. When she returned a few minutes later he noticed tears in her eyes.

"My husband was a good policeman" she said.

"Yes, ma'am, I'm sure he. . ."

"He was shot in the leg, in one of those ambushes he mentioned."

"So that's why he limps, because he was wounded, because. . ."

"He could have retired disabled, but he loved police work."

"But now he thinks they. . ."

"In the thirties, the Depression, they helped a lot of poor people then."

"But now he thinks they're taking bribes?"

"In East Austin, that and worse things, too. He's sure of it. So am I."

She took the pictures from the wall, the photographs Dee had said he could use with the story he would write. As she removed them from their frames and put them in an envelope he was not sure what to say. Not sure what he would write.

"East Austin" he said. "I'll look into it, ma'am, but. . ."

"You know what's odd, Mister Dee?"

"Odd? No, I. . ."

"Your paper never prints a word about East Austin."

As he stood on the sidewalk outside their home, ready to walk a mile to work, Dee looked back and saw her standing on the porch. Trembley's wife, waving farewell and nodding. As if she expected him to do it, to report what her husband had called the paper about. Police corruption, rigging votes, taking bribes and worse.

Two old people, maybe dreaming it up, afraid the world has gone to hell in their old age. Like his granddad in West Texas, before he died, spitting out tobacco juice and muttering about how Roosevelt had conspired to start the Depression.

Dreaming it up. Maybe. But Trembley's wife, she's right about one thing. The paper, never a word in the paper about East Austin. Odd. Damned odd, at that, come to think about it.

Sunday afternoon, on his one day off at the paper, Dee found an empty table at the Split Rail tavern and sat down. Gazing at the Colorado River and the hills beyond. Watching the birds fly over. Peaceful, outdoors, in the shade under a thatched roof, a quiet place to study.

"Phil, what'll it be?" asked the bartender. "How about a bottle of Lone Star?"

"And some French fries, to go with this French book."

"Quite a story, what you wrote about that old policeman and his wife."

"I left out a lot. Some things I wasn't sure about."

"The Comanches, I never knew they got that close to Austin."

"You read that part about the bootleggers who shot Trembley?"

"Bastards. Like that one over there with your buddy from the paper."

Dee looked where the bartender was pointing. To Ashley, the city editor, drinking beer with a man Dee had never seen. Fine, he had French to work on. And other things to think about.

He opened his book, trying to find the word for cheerleaders. Avoir bon espoir, to be of good cheer, as close as he could come. Not close enough, nowhere near that blonde haired teaser Debbie Decker and her pals.

"Phil, put that book down" he heard Ashley say and looked up. "Come over here and join us, I want you to meet an old friend from Indiana." Dee got up. Why not? One more week, he'd be finished with the French class, he could throw the book away.

"Abraham Liebwitz" said the man as he shook Dee's hand. "Call me Abe."

"Abe it is" said Dee and sat down, waving to the bartender to bring his glass over here. Looking at Liebwitz, somewhere in his forties, thick black hair, wearing a Tee shirt with the words Brush Your Teeth With Pepsodent on it.

"Abe's a dentist" said Ashley.

"Passing through on business" said Abe.

"Go on" said Ashley. "You were talking about the University."

"The law school" said Abe. "The way they've treated that Negro kid."

"First one they admitted" said Ashley. "Folks here, they're not used to that."

"So they put railings around where he sits. Right, Amos?"

"Yes, in all the law school classes he's in, I have to admit."

"Railings, to keep him separate from the white kids. I'd call that dumb.".

"Down here, that's called segregation" said Ashley. "Look around you."

"What do you think?" asked Abe, turning to Dee. "What would you call it?"

"Don't drag me into this" said Dee. "But if you really want to know, I'd call it bullshit." He got up and started to walk away. Annoyed. Toward the Split Rail bar, stopping when he heard Ashley calling out.

"Come back" he said. "Abe didn't mean to upset you."

"I'm not upset" said Dee. "I've got other things on my mind."

"He's at the University" said Ashley. "He's trying to graduate."

"Sit down" said Abe. "Amos told me you're one of his reporters."

"I am, he has me on the police beat right now."

"The police. You have much crime in Austin?"

"Burglary, a murder now and then, the police keep things under control."

"Murders. The police, they commit the murders, do they?"

"I didn't say that. Why are you twisting my words?"

"When the police murder someone, do you report on that?"

Dee did not reply. Looking at Liebwitz across the table. Just as the bartender warned, a bastard, all right. Telling him out loud "No, young man, I don't think you do" as he stood up, leaning on a cane, looking at Dee and shaking his head.

"Calm down" said Ashley. "Leave him alone, Abe."

"See what my shirt says" Liebwitz sneered. "Brush Your Teeth With Pepsodent. On the radio, have you heard the rest of that commercial?"

Dee did not reply. Of course he'd heard. Who hadn't? On every radio station, all day long. So what? To hell with Pepsodent. To hell with this dentist, to.

"Brush your teeth with Pepsodent, you will wonder where the yellow went" said Liebwitz. "Where the yellow went, that's the rest of it."

Silence for a moment, Dee looking up at Liebwitz and wondering, Ashley lowering his head, Liebwitz looking down at Dee and sneering.

"That goes for you" he said. "You're like all the rest, you're yellow."

He hobbled away then, cursing, out of the Split Rail, using his cane as a crutch. With Ashley behind him, saying something, patting Liebwitz on the back, guiding him to a car in the parking lot.

Dee got up and went to the bar. Another Lone Star, he told the bartender, I've just had a go-round with that bastard. You tagged him right. See him, getting in his car? If he comes around again, give him a shot of rat poison and put it on my bill.

"Rat poison" said the bartender. "Maybe you'd better pay in advance."

"Pay for what? This one's on me" said Ashley over his shoulder.

"Amos, leave me alone" said Dee. "I've had enough."

"What Abe said, I know, Phil, but he's a fried, he. . ."

"A friend. You heard what he called me? Yellow."

"I know, I know, but. . ."

"And Liebwitz is your friend? Amos, leave me alone."

"What he said, about you, about the police, all right, I heard, but. . ."

Dee walked away, back to the table he'd been sitting at before. With his book and his beer in hand. Ashley followed and stood beside him for a moment. "Get up" he said. "Let's go for a ride."

Dee looked up. Ashley, impatient all at once, in no mood to tangle with now. And still his boss. Dee got up. "Where to?" he asked.

"I want to show you something" said Ashley. "And I want to tell you something about police."

Police. Liebwitz had already told him something about police. That he was too yellow to report what they did.

Maybe he was. Or maybe not. He wasn't sure.

They drove past the past the pitch and putt golf course next to the Split Rail, past the baseball stadium, empty, with the team out of town. Past Congress and on to First Street. Ashley, steering his way through Sunday traffic. With something on his mind. Thinking, finally speaking.

"Abe and me, we grew up together. Indiana, in the twenties."

"So he's a dentist now. And you're a city editor. Fine."

"We got in a fight one time. Over my father."

"Your father? What about him?"

"He was in the Ku Klux Klan. You know about the Klan, Phil?"

Dee rubbed the side of his face, recalling what he'd read. The Klan, bad news, almost gone, sprouting up again during Prohibition, throughout Indiana, buying state politicians, going after Catholics and Jews as well as Negroes.

"Amos, your dad belonged to the Klan? How old were you?"

"Only a kid. The white robes, I had no idea what they meant."

"Burning crosses, you didn't know what that meant?"

"Abe knew. His dad was a lawyer in the town we grew up in."

"The Klan, I'll be damned. That fight you mentioned, what happened then?"

"One month later they shot his dad, right on Abe's front porch."

Dee looked at Ashley. Wondering if he should ask what happened to his own dad. Wondering if he knew Ashley at all. Never talking about himself before, for some reason opening up now about his father.

Ashley, with his feet propped on his desk, going through the paper every day, with that grease pencil in his hand, marking stories, God only knows what else he'd kept buried from his past.

"That town, Phil, the police, they all belonged to the Klan."

"All right, Amos, there's something else you're trying to tell me. What is it?"

"Abe knew the police killed his dad, that's what I'm telling you."

"And the paper there, they kept it quiet, that's what you're getting at, too."

"Not a word. I was grown up before I knew what had happened."

He swerved to dodge an oncoming car, honking its horn, the driver yelling watch where you're going. No wonder. Ashley's mind was somewhere else. Indiana in the twenties. No point in warning about his driving. Just hang on and keep listening.

"Amos, that's ancient history, why are you telling me this now?"

"So you can understand why Abe got on your ass."

"Because a newspaper let him down? Thirty years ago?"

"We're still letting him down. Abe thinks I'm yellow, too."

Ashley turned on to East Avenue, driving up a hill to Rosewood Avenue, looking for a place to park. When he found one they got out, saw a sign saying Parade Route No Parking After 3, and got back in. Ashley drove on, still talking.

"By the way, my dad wasn't there when they shot Abe's father."

"I was wondering, Amos, sure. . ."

"He was out of town, locked up in Kentucky on a bootlegging charge."

"Some father you had. What happened after that?"

"I have no idea, Phil, we never saw him again."

No luck finding a place to part off Rosewood, either. The side streets were jammed with cars. Negroes getting out, carrying umbrellas and folding chairs, ready to watch a parade, it looked like.

"This part of town, Phil, you've been here, I suppose."

"Late at night, there's a place where we eat sometimes, what about it?"

"The people downtown, you know what they call it?"

"East Austin? Sure, I've heard some other names. Nigger town, for one."

Ashley turned off a side street, driving along an alley behind Rosewood, to the loading zone in back of a two story wooden building. With a sign over the screen door entrance in the rear. Lucky Bubba's Fried Chitlins.

"That's his pick up" he said, pointing to a truck in the loading zone.

"Amos, I don't have time for this, I need to study French."

"Not French. What you need to study is Texas history."

"The Alamo, sure, I know, I know..."

"Forget the Alamo. What day is it? The date, I mean."

"The date? Sunday, the nineteenth of June, so what?"

"Juneteenth, that's what it's called in this part of town."

"Look, they can call it whatever they like, I need to. . ."

"You'll see, Phil. That's why I brought you here. Juneteenth."

Dee got out of the car, following Ashley. Looking back in the alley. Piles of cardboard boxes, stray dogs sniffing in the trash barrels behind a row of wooden buildings. Run down. East Austin. A different part of town.

"Bubba, are you in there?" Ashley yelled through the screen door.

"Why does he call himself Lucky?" asked Dee as they waited.

"In France, he made it out when a bomb hit his truck" said Ashley. He glanced at his watch and yelled a second time. Still no answer. Dee looked up at the sign again. Lucky Bubba's Fried Chitlins. Not so lucky now, cooking crap like that.

"Mister Amos, come on in" a woman finally answered.

Ashley opened the screen door and went in, Dee behind him. Into a room with a half dozen tables, a heavy set Negro woman coming from the entrance to a kitchen, and the smell of barbecue in the air.

"Miss Jeffreys, meet a friend of mine" said Ashley. "Phillip Dee."

"Miss Jeffreys, that's what Amos calls me" said the woman, looking at Dee, smiling, wiping her apron and shaking hands. "That ain't what Bubba calls me. To him I'm plain old Lady Bubba."

"That's for the initials, Phil" said Ashley. "Lady Bubba Jeffreys. LBJ."

"Senator Johnson" said the woman. "I declare, my husband do worship that man."

"Bubba, where is he?" asked Ashley.

"Back there" she answered. "I'll get him. He ain't doin' too good."

The Negro man who came from the kitchen was on crutches, with one of his ankles in a cast. Short, a bandage around his head, wearing an old Army uniform. Holding on to the crutches, trying to shake hands with Dee as Ashley introduced him..

"Bubba, what happened to you?" asked Ashley. "Some kind of accident?"

"I guess you might call it that" he answered, nodding, speaking softly.

"Too bad you can't march" said Ashley. "You'll have to watch with us."

"In a while. You ever seen this parade, Mister Dee?"

"First time" he answered, looking at Bubba's uniform. Four ribbons and corporal's stripes on his blouse. Behind him, on the wall, an American flag, ripped apart and sewn back together, with stitches down the middle.

"We'll put some chairs out so you can watch" said Bubba.

"Juneteenth" said Ashley. "Phil doesn't know what it is."

"Ninety years ago today" said Bubba. "That's when they let the slaves go."

"The parade" said Dee. "That's what it's for?"

"It's s'posed to be" said Bubba. "Sometimes I wonder." As he spoke he looked at the flag on the wall, then hobbled back to the kitchen. In a moment Lady Bubba came out with two glasses of iced tea and placed them on a table.

"Sit down, Phil" said Ashley. "There's more than what he told you."

"Slaves" said Dee. "I know, Texas was a slave state back then."

"The Civil War, it ended in an April, you must know that, too."

"So . . . wait . . . they didn't free the slaves down here until June?"

"The Union Army, Phil, they kept it secret from them."

"Why? What for? The war was over, they were free, they. . ."

"So they'd finish the cotton crop first" said Ashley. "Ask Bubba, his grandfather was a slave near Waco."

Dee looked down at his glass and brushed a fly away. Ashley got up and went to the kitchen. Through the entrance Dee could see him talking with Bubba. When he returned with a fly swatter and sat down he was shaking his head.

"Damn it, I don't believe it" said Ashley. "He's too tough for that."

"Who, Bubba? Too tough for what? He's on crutches."

"That accident, how it happened, I asked him just now. He won't tell me."

"Hell, Amos, maybe he fell down, maybe he won't admit it."

"No, I know him too well for that. He's hiding something, Phil."

Whatever it was, he came from the kitchen a few minutes later, with Lady Bubba behind him, telling her to put some chairs on the sidewalk. Not easy. The front door was off its hinges, too big to push aside.

Ashley got up, Dee beside him, and they lifted the door. Heavy, wooden, split and broken down the middle. They leaned the door against the wall, turned around, and looked at Lady Bubba, pushing a chair through a curtain covering the entrance.

"Wait" said Dee. "Leave the chairs to us, what happened to your door?"

"It got broke" she said. "The same night Bubba had his accident."

"What happened?" asked Ashley. "He won't tell me."

"If he won't, I ain't, neither" she said. Turning around when she heard a voice behind them. A young Negro girl, coming from upstairs, holding a baby in her arms, fanning it with a folded newspaper while she looked out a window.

"Papa, it's time for the parade" she said. "Let's go sit outside."

"My daughter Lola Bird" said Bubba. "You know her, Mister Amos."

A round of greetings then, Ashley asking how old the baby was, Lola Bird saying three months, he's a sweet potato, Dee pushing chairs through the curtain, hearing the sound of a band coming up Rosewood, sitting down with the others to watch.

A truck came first. A flatbed, with a plywood sign on top, the year 1865 painted in huge black numbers. In the rear, bales of cotton, a dozen young Negro boys and girls in coveralls, throwing white fluff in the air, acting like they were picking cotton.

Behind the truck, not far back, two men carrying a banner mounted on poles. Red and blue, with the words Huston-Tillotson College on it, and a Latin slogan Dee had trouble making sense of.

And then the College band. Led by a drum major twirling a baton. Marching to the beat of a song about slaves, a jazzed up version of Old Man River. Trumpets and trombones blaring away, the crowd on the sidewalk cheering as the band moved on.

"Look at 'em strut" said Lady Bubba. "Ain't they somethin'?"

"You should see how they do it in Detroit" said Ashley.

"They have parades like this up there?" asked Dee.

"All over" answered Ashley. "Fifty, sixty years ago, when Texas Negroes moved up North to work, they took it with them. Juneteenth, Phil." Dee looked at Ashley and nodded. One more thing he had never heard about.

As the band marched on he watched what followed. A pink convertible, open, with a young Negro woman sitting on top in the back, wearing some sort of crown, waving to the crowd. This year's parade queen, it looked like.

Dee stood up as the car went by, offering his seat to a Negro woman. With a baby in her arms. Ashley did the same for another one. Dee looked around. Two whites, all the others black, waving paper American flags on sticks and cheering.

Another band then. Lincoln High School. Followed by three more convertibles with the tops down. In the last one a tall white man in the back seat, all alone, looking straight ahead. Greeted with silence.

"Who's that?" asked Dee.

"Congressman Lomax" said Ashley. "East Austin is part of his district."

"Looks like this crowd doesn't like him."

"Maybe not, but they sure as hell vote for him, that's how he gets elected."

The cheering erupted again once the cars went by. Behind them, a color guard, four Negro men in Army uniforms, the two in the middle carrying flags, the one on the right the American flag, the one on the left a green flag with the number 64 on it.

Dee held his hand over his chest and stood at attention. A company of Negroes, thirty or forty, all in uniform, trying to keep in step. Led by a man with sergeant's stripes, looking over his shoulder and yelling "Straighten up, look sharp for Bubba."

The end of the parade. The crowd on the sidewalk moved out on the street and followed, still cheering. "They be goin' to the park now" said Lady Bubba. "We be takin' barbecue for the pick nick."

With that she started pushing chairs through the curtains, Dee and Ashley and her daughter Lola Bird helping, Bubba hobbling to the kitchen. The door came next. Five minutes at least to push it back in the frame and close it.

"The carpenter's coming tomorrow, he'll fix it" said Bubba as he came from the kitchen. Leaning on his crutches, offering Ashley a paper sack. "Some barbecue sandwiches, Mister Amos, if you don't want to go to the park."

"Thanks, no sandwiches" said Ashley. "But we'll help load your truck."

"Linus, he can drive it" said Bubba. "He's at the college right now."

"Linus, who's that?" asked Dee.

"My son in law" Bubba answered. "He's studying to be a lawyer."

"Bubba, I'd still like to know" said Ashley. "What happened to. . ."

"Mister Phil, you like barbecue? Come by some night, we'll fix you a plate."

"Barbecue, fine" said Dee. But please, no chitlins."

"Me neither" said Bubba. "Pig guts. In the Army, we'd shoot a cook for that."

Dee went to the kitchen and helped Ashley carry boxes to the truck out back. Barbecue sandwiches for a picnic in the park. Juneteenth. One more thing to know about. One more thing to study. Texas history.

"Wait" said Ashley as they started to drive away. He turned off the engine and got out of the car. "That's Linus, what's wrong with him?"

Dee got out and looked. A young Negro man, coming down the alley. Neat, wearing sunglasses, dressed in a coat and tie, his hair greased back with pomade. His left arm in a sling, holding a book satchel with his right hand.

"Linus, what happened to you?" asked Ashley.

"The police, they broke my wrist" he answered. "Bubba didn't tell you?"

"No, he wouldn't say. The police, they broke his ankle, too?"

"They were drunk, he told them we were closed, but they wouldn't listen."

"The door, what happened, they broke it open?"

"More than that. They ripped down his flag and threw him on the floor."

"You tried to stop them and they broke your wrist, is that it?"

"Hard to study now, but at least I can drive. Who's this with you, Amos?"

Dee stepped forward and introduced himself. Linus set his book satchel on the ground and shook hands. Then he picked it up, tossed it in the front seat of the truck and looked in the rear, where the boxes had been loaded.

"I have to go" he said. "I'm driving them to the park."

"Hang on" said Dee. "I'd like to ask a question, Linus."

"Phil's on the paper" said Ashley. "He's on the police beat."

"Police" said Linus. "Screw the police."

"These two cops who did this" said Dee. "Can you identify them?"

"Mid twenties, maybe, mean as hell."

"What else? Did you see their name plates?"

"Sure, the names on their jackets."

"Good, the names, what were they?"

"You must be out of your mind" answered Linus, turning his back on Dee and walking into the café, slamming the screen door behind him. Ashley got in his car, started the engine, motioned to Dee to get in, and they drove off.

"That was dumb" said Ashley. "You should have known Linus wouldn't tell you." Dee did not reply. As they drove out of the alley he watched the crowd on Rosewood, still celebrating Juneteenth. And nodded.

Ashley turned on to East Avenue, down to First Street, crossing Congress without a word. Neither of them speaking until he stopped at the baseball stadium, pulled into a parking lot, and turned off the engine.

"Baseball" he said. "You know who Jackie Robinson is?"

"Sure" Dee answered. "The first Negro player in the majors."

"Before that, did you know he coached at Tillotson College?"

"Robinson? He was here? In Austin?"

"No, of course you wouldn't know, it was never in the paper."

Ashley got out and leaned against a fender, looking at the stadium. Dee stood beside him, looking back at Congress Street. At the dome of the Texas state capitol. Wondering how much he knew about Texas. About the paper.

"Juneteenth" said Ashley. "We won't print that, either."

"Why not?" asked Dee. "Who's this we you're talking about?"

"The front office. That's the policy, we don't cover Negroes."

"What happens to Negroes, that's off limits? Why?"

"You ask why? My God, you really are dumb, Phil."

Ashley walked away then, toward the pitch and putt course near the Split Rail, with his hands folded behind him. Staring off in the distance. After a while he came back and leaned against the fender again. Silent. Bothered about something.

"All right, Amos, I'm dumb. I should not have asked Linus about the cops."

"Go ahead, talk about it, tell me why Linus would not ID them."

"He's afraid they'd come back, I guess. They might. . ."

"Might what, Phil? Burn the place down?"

"Arson? Set Bubba's place on fire? I don't know, I. . ."

"Not arson, bad wiring, that's what the fire department would say."

"Amos, that's too much, you really believe that?"

"Burn it down, Phil, with Bubba and his whole damned family inside."

Ashley stood away from the car. Pacing back and forth. Looking down at the gravel parking lot. Shaking his head, trying to make up his mind about something, it seemed. Whatever it was, Dee had never seen him act like this.

"Bubba, he was damned near forty when he enlisted" said Ashley.

"That old? He enlisted, he wasn't drafted?"

"The Sixty Fourth Quartermaster Company, I've seen the records."

"The police, they should leave him alone then, they should. . ."

"A Bronze Star and a Purple Heart. You saw what the police did."

"Amos, look, let me dig into this, let me. . ."

"Dig into it, hell. They could burn his place down, with his family inside, and we wouldn't report that, either. The front office, that's the policy, Phil."

He got in the car and started the engine. Slow, shifting gears to back out, adjusting the rear view mirror, looking at himself in the mirror, shaking his head. While Dee reached for his book in the back seat.

"Where to?" asked Ashley. "The Split Rail? Home, to study French?"

"Home, if you will, and listen, I've been thinking, Amos."

"What about? Juneteenth, what the cops did to Bubba?"

"About the front office, that policy you mentioned. A way to get around it."

Ashley listened, driving on as Dee spelled it out. Tie the police reports together, in a daily summary, not in separate stories. With no mention of Negroes at first, only the incident. Then slowly, month by month, add the location, see if the front office even catches on, see how the policy stands up.

"We can try it, Phil. Sure, put it all together. Call it the Blotter."

"If they do catch on, what can they do? Fire us both?"

"Maybe, but to hell with that. Not a bad idea, Phil."

"Not bad? You know what that is in French? Pas mal, Amos, pas mal."

"Pas mal? So what's the French word for yellow?"

"Yellow, I don't know, I. . ."

"Look it up. Maybe we're not so damned yellow, after all."

"Jaune. I just remembered, jaune, that's the word for yellow."

"Jaune? Good. Don't worry, you're going to pass that French course, Phil."

When Ashley dropped him off Dee walked into the courtyard on Lorraine Street, stopped for a moment, and shook his head. The Blotter, fine, call it that, see if the big brass catches on.

Or call it Gendarmes, isn't that the French word for police? Maybe then they wouldn't even notice.

Amos was right. Don't worry. Don't worry about a damned thing. The Blotter, Gendarmes, it doesn't matter. Just go study and keep your fingers crossed.

DUMB BELLES

IN LATE AUGUST DEE STOOD IN FRONT OF A BULLETIN BOARD and braced himself. With his fingers crossed. Looking for his grade in French. Holding his breath. The initials P.D. If they were there, he passed. The failing grades were never listed.

"D plus" he yelled out loud. "Thank the Lord, I'm done."

"Please step aside" he heard a female voice demand. "You are blocking my view." The coed with the red hair, jewelry and all, with her hands on her hips, looking at the bulletin board as if she owned it. And then at Dee, as if she owned him, too.

"It's you again" she said. "Did I hear you say D plus?"

"You heard right" he answered. "What about it?"

"Just what I'd expect, from a tramp who delivers papers."

Dee looked down at his khaki trousers. Dirty, smudged on the knees. From falling down, in the touch football game he had just played in, on the lawn across from the gym, with a dozen others waiting for grades to be posted. None of her business.

"Wait" she said as he started to walk away.

"What for? You want to show me the A you got in Spanish?"

"No, I want to look at you."

She did. Stepping back, removing her reading glasses, her eyes running up and down his clothes, from his shoes to his shirt and the top of his head. Dee reached up, felt a twig of grass in his hair and removed it. Annoyed by the look on her face.

"Yes" she said, in a voice of disdain. "I believe you will do."

"Do what? Deliver the paper to your front door?"

"I would like you to take me to our tea dance."

"You must be joking. A tea dance? What's that?"

"You will see. What is your name?"

"Phillip Dee. What's yours?"

She put her glasses on, reached in her purse, and handed him a card. Engraved. Dee looked at the card. Meredith Ogletree, Kappa Gamma Gamma. A sorority princess, inviting him to a dance? More than odd. Damned odd.

"My number is on the card" she said. "Call me and say yes or no."

"Call you? I don't understand, I. . ."

"I'm sure you don't. You'll be perfect."

"Perfect for what?"

"The dance is Saturday. Call me, I must know tomorrow."

She walked away then. Smiling. Dee looked at the card again. And back to the bulletin board as she disappeared. The Spanish grades. M.O. Meredith Ogletree. An A, all right. One minute sneering at him, the next minute smiling. Weird.

The clerk in the bookstore across the street thought it was more than weird. When Dee placed his French text on the counter, ready to sell it back, and asked if he knew what a tea dance might be.

"You don't know?" said the clerk. "What fraternity are you in?"

"None" Dee answered. "So what is it?"

"Sorority shit. You got invited, and you're not in a fraternity?"

"That's right. What's the book worth?"

"A dollar. Fellow, somebody's pulling your leg."

"No, look at this card, that's who asked me."

"Kappa Gamma Gamma, damn, they're the richest babes on campus."

Dee put the dollar in his pocket. Hearing the clerk say "I don't get it" as he walked outside, to the bus stop on Guadalupe. Heading home to change clothes and get to work at the paper. A tea dance? With a rich sorority babe? Hard to believe.

At half past three Ashley came to his desk, holding a sheet of paper. Dee's first take of the day for The Blotter. With more to come in the hours ahead. One paragraph reports on police actions around Austin, each with a short headline.

"Good" said Ashley. "Car crash on Rosewood. Keep it simple."

"No mention of Negroes" said Dee.

"What's this last one? Police investigate University grades?"

"An inside job, no other way to explain it."

"You passed your French course? Strange way to tell me.'"

"Passed, barely. Go ahead, cross it out, it's a joke."

"Grow up, jokes are for the amusement page your buddy edits."

"Parker, where is he? I need to see him, I've got a problem, Amos."

"At the Paramount, watching a movie. Wake him up, he has problems, too."

No need to wake him up. He was coming from the Paramount when Dee crossed over Congress. Standing under the marquee. The High And The Nighty, the movie title, Dee noticed as he followed Parker. To the Driskill Hotel, into the coffee shop. Where he was sitting at a table, scribbling in a notepad.

"Steve, I've got a question" said Dee.

"You want to know why I'm working in here, is that it?"

"No, it's something else, it's. . ."

"I'm just trying to stay away from Buck, that's all."

"Look, it's not about Buck, it's. . ."

"He's been on my ass, ever since that crap about the noise."

"I know, the noise at our place, but. . ."

"Ever since he squeezed it out of me, why the cops wouldn't stop it."

"That one policeman, he was an Army pal, I know."

"Buck had him moved to another route, what about him?"

"Not about him, Steve. Fraternities. Sororities. Here, look at this."

Dee handed him the card from Meredith Ogletree. And spelled it out with questions. A tea dance, she's invited him, why, when he doesn't belong in that crowd? A sorority bash of some sort, what's she up to? Most of all, could it be for real?

"Kappa Gamma Gamma" said Parker, looking at the card. "Not likely."

"So why would she. . ."

"Look, I have to write about this damned John Wayne movie."

"Steve, I need to know. What's she up to?"

"Hell, I don't know, but all right, there's a way to find out."

"How? You know someone in that sorority?"

"That dress shop across the street. Come on, I'll write this later."

Parker folded his notes and led him to the dress shop. Expensive, Dee had seen a week before. When he bought a silk scarf for ten dollars, with money Buck coughed up from his slush fund. A gift to Hattie for a tip about some crooked cops to watch for.

"Julie Trenton, she's the owner" said Parker as he led him in.

"I've met her" said Dee. "She belonged to that sorority?"

"Still does. Let's see what Julie knows about this shit."

She was at the counter. An elegant blonde, Parker's age, selling a dress to an older woman. When she saw Parker she smiled, told an assistant to wrap the dress, and came from behind the counter. Dee stood aside and listened.

"Steve" she said. "I'm still waiting for that dinner you promised."

"As soon as I get paid, Julie. Right now, it's about my friend Phil."

She nodded when Parker handed her the sorority card. Yes, Dee heard her say, Meredith, she's the Gamma Gamma president now, if you like, come in my office, Steve, I'll call her and find out, but keep your hands to yourself, it's business hours.

Dee waited. For ten minutes. Looking at the price tags on the dresses. Fifty dollars. A hundred dollars. Wondering, if Hattie came up with another tip, whether Buck would fork over that much money. Maybe, if it could put the mayor in jail.

No need to wonder about the tea dance, not with the look on her face when Julie came out of her office. Frowning, with Parker behind her, as she returned the card to Dee and shook her head.

"Skip this dance" she said. "Meredith plans to make a fool of you."

"Why? Because I got a D in French? She must be. . ."

"She's had a trophy made. A dumb bell."

"A dumb bell? She's that mean, she'd do that to me?"

"If not you, someone else she finds. It's her idea of fun."

"Fun? She's so uppity she would. . ."

"Uppity? That's why she let me in on this, to brag about it."

"Bragging, she must think I'm an idiot, if she. . ."

"Perhaps she does. All I can say is skip it."

She went back to her office, with Parker behind her, and closed the door. Perhaps to help him write his movie review. Or something like that. Dee smiled. When he reached the corner he looked back at the Paramount marquee, still smiling. The High And The Mighty.

"You think you're high, Miss Meredith" he said out loud, still smiling. "You bitch, Saturday, by God, you want some fun, we'll see how mighty you are."

Calls to make. Four, by Dee's count. First, the desk sergeant at the precinct, to bring The Blotter up to speed. Next, the bank, to see if there's enough to cover Saturday. And the last two calls, the most important of all. To get things rolling.

"Looks slow so far" said Ashley when Dee handed him his next take.

"One burglary, one stolen car. Amos, do you know what a dumb bell is?"

"A piece of iron, for weight lifting. You figure you need some muscles?"

"Maybe, when I finish this. It's for Steve's amusement page."

"Stop making jokes. You don't get paid to write that trash."

Dee went back to work, pounding away on his typewriter. Not trash. A plan, for Parker to help with. Step by step, all the details, right down to the Sunday headline and a picture. Miss Meredith, with that dumb bell shoved in her face.

"Eighty six dollars and nineteen cents" said the teller on the phone, when Dee asked how much was left in his account. Not much, but enough. Next, the directory from the University, the number for Debbie Decker, see if she's home.

"It's Omar" he said when she answered.

"You? What do you want, you need some entertaining?"

"No, Debbie, it's your car, I want to rent it."

"With me in the rumble seat? No way, it's still daylight."

"No, no, listen. Saturday, noon, without you. Ten dollars, Debbie."

"You're cute, Omar, but you're crazy. You can have it for five."

Dee made a mark on his checklist, looked at the sorority card, nodded, and dialed the number. Holding his breath. Remembering how the voices sometimes sounded in East Texas. Dumb and illiterate.

"Kappa Gamma Gama" a female answered. "May I ask who is calling?"

"This here's Phillip Dee. I need to speak at Meredith."

"Yes, she's expecting your call. Please wait, she's playing tennis."

Expecting his call? Strange, when she said he should let her know tomorrow. Dee waited, hearing female voices, faint, muffled, someone holding a hand over the phone. When she finally spoke, Meredith sounded uneasy.

"Have you talked to Julie Trenton?"

"Trinity? Julia Trinity?" Dee responded, stalling for time.

"She has a shop downtown, do you know her?"

"Downtown, that ain't on my route, I don't deliver downtown."

A pause then, neither speaking. Dee relaxed, pleased he had dodged a bullet. So she'd been worried Julie had warned him, fine, when he was finished with her, Miss Meredith would have a lot more to worry about.

"Very well" she said. "What have you decided?"

"About that there tea dance? I'm rarin' to go."

"Yes, I imagine you are. Be here Saturday at two."

"That's where we're dancin'? That sorty house on Lamar?"

"No, you idiot, the dance is at Lake Austin."

"You bet, but you gotta promise not to step on my toes."

No reply. Only a click as she hung up the phone. Back to work then. Finish the plan. Show it to Parker, typing away in the corner with his movie review. Give him his copy, get him to buy off on what Dee would need him to do.

"You're off the wall" said Parker when he read the sheet Dee handed him.

"Steve, you have to take Julie, that's your cover for being there."

"So I can write about this shit? Damned clever."

"Get one of the guys from the darkroom, we'll need a picture, too."

"For the Sunday paper? No way, that page is locked up two days before."

"Tell Jake you'll give him ten bucks to redo it, it has to be Sunday."

"Where's this money coming from? You're renting a tux? That's another ten."

"Damned right, a tuxedo. A tuxxy do do, for that there sorty girl."

"Not bad, Phil, that sound's like some dumb farmer, all right. Count me in."

"One last thing. Don't tell Julie what I'm up to. She might spill it."

Dee went back to his desk. Back to work on The Blotter. Smiling as he looked at the phone book. Adding one more call to his list. Big John's Pawn Shop. Talk him into being open Saturday afternoon. Ten dollars for ten minutes, Big John will leap on that.

A pawn shop, that should really do her in.

She was standing on the porch of her sorority house when Dee drove up. Meredith, along with a half dozen other coeds, all of them dressed like queens, waiting for their dates to escort them to the tea dance.

Dee got out of Debbie's beat up coupe, straightened the tux he had rented, and went to the rumble seat, shoving aside a stack of newspapers, slowly, so they could see. As he closed the seat he reached in the front for a bouquet of flowers, hearing them laugh.

"Look at that suit" said one. "I wonder where he found that."

"The same place he found that wreck he's driving" a second coed answered.

"My goodness, Meredith" said another. "You do know how to pick them."

"A delivery boy" said another coed. "You should be ashamed of yourself."

"I'm not" she said. "Wait until you hear how he talks."

"Howdy" said Dee. "I brung you some purty flowers."

"You see what I mean?" said Meredith to the others, taking the flowers and shaking her head. Dee opened the car door and stood aside, bowing, acting like a gentleman, pushing some papers under the seat, while the coeds on the porch went on laughing.

"Hop in, Miss Mary, let's go to this here dance."

"Please, my name is not Mary. My name is Meredith Ogletree."

"Ogletree, yes ma'am, I been meanin' to ask. What kind of tree is that?"

She groaned without answering. Looking down at the flowers in her lap. Pansies, twenty cents worth, fresh from a grocery. Dee drove away, looking back at the coeds on the porch, still laughing. Fine, in an hour or two they would all be groaning, like her.

"Where are you going?" she asked. "This is not the way to Lake Austin."

"I gotta make a stop first" Dee answered. "Somethin' to pick up."

"Really. Then stop some place where they sell cigarettes."

"You want a chew? I got some Red Dog under the seat."

"Red Dog? Chewing tobacco? You must be. . ."

"It ain't bad. You gotta be careful you don't swallow."

A good thing she did not ask to see, since there was no Red Dog under the seat. Best to stop ad libbing. Stick to the plan. Stopping for cigarettes, a minor delay, Dee calculated, as he parked in front of a service station and followed her in.

"I would like a package of Parliaments" she said to the man in the station.

"Parliaments . . . let me see" he said as he reached for a box under the counter.

"What's in that box?" she demanded to know.

"Lady, I got Trojans, and some rubber things from Mexico, but. . ."

"My God! My God!" she screamed and went running to the car.

"What's wrong?" the man asked. "That kind, they got some special tingle?"

"Parliaments are cigarettes" said Dee. "We'll settle for Chesterfields."

Dee handed him five dollars, said keep the change, you earned it, and went to the car. When he gave her the Chesterfields he noticed she was blushing, her face almost as red as her hair. Parliaments and the box under the counter. Never, ever, could he have cooked up something quite so charming.

She was silent as he drove on. Slumped down in her seat, staring at the flowers under her feet, smoking, coming unglued, it looked like. Too early for that. He would have to be careful when he got to Big John's.

"A pawn shop?" she asked. "Why are we stopping here?"

"I need a couple of bucks for gas. Wait here."

Inside the shop he handed Big John a ten dollar bill, two ones, and a sheet of paper. Saying take a few minutes, when I go back to the car, come out and do what's on that sheet, and keep a straight face, it's the easiest ten you ever made.

Big John read the sheet and nodded. Dee glanced at a clock on the wall. Right on schedule. He went back to the car, got in, looked at Meredith and muttered "That ole man, he's a tightwad, all I asked was. . ."

"Wait" said Big John, running out to the car. "I've changed my mind."

"Two bucks" said Dee. "I ain't gonna settle for less."

"Your mother's wrist watch, it's not worth it, but here's two dollars."

"All righty, it's a deal" said Dee. "That'll sure pay for the gas I need."

"Your mother's wrist watch, my God" groaned Meredith.

Dee started the engine, turned around, and drove on. Back to Lamar, on the way to Lake Austin. Reaching down to the gas gauge, tapping with his finger, watching Meredith light another cigarette.

"Gas?" she asked. "You don't have enough gas?"

"I got enough to get us there" he answered. "It's for later."

"Later? What do you mean, later?"

"After this here dance, sure, drive around and park some place."

"My God, you must be out of your mind if you think. . ."

"Hanky panky, ain't that what you wanted them Parliaments for?"

Good, that did it, even if it was another ad lib, tying it all together. She was ready to smack him in the face, embarrassed, no doubt mad as hell, in the perfect mood for what comes next. A lesson for Miss Meredith. What counts as fun.

"Let me out in front, right now" she ordered as he drove into the parking lot outside the night club where the dance was being held. Dee nodded. Fine, do whatever Meredith says. Until it's dumb bell time. Then she's on her own.

She opened the car door and leaped out, stumbling, reaching down to pick up one of her high heels, putting it on again, looking around to see if anyone had noticed how she tripped, straightening her dress, prancing into the night club entrance by herself.

Dee found a parking place, amid of a row of limousines, and smiled at the way the coupe with the rumble seat matched up. No place for a poor delivery boy. A sign above the doorway said the rest. Reserved for Kappa Gamma Gamma.

A quick look around to check the layout. A bar with three men serving drinks, an orchestra playing soft music, twenty or thirty couples dancing, Parker with Julie in his arms, Meredith in the corner with another coed, looking in a cardboard box and nodding.

Dee went to the bar. To one of the three men serving drinks.

"All set, Rudy?" he asked.

"All set. My Speed Graphic's behind this case of beer."

"Make it good, one shot, that's all you'll get."

"One shot. Where the hell did you find that suit?"

"It's for her. For this coed who dragged me here."

"Watch out, she's right behind you, Phil."

Dee turned around and looked at Meredith. Noticing at once how different she seemed. Composed. In charge of things, now that she was in the dance hall with her friends, no longer in the car with him. Acting coy, taking his hand.

"One dance, that's all" she said. "Let's see if you know how."

They walked together onto the dance floor. All alone, the others standing aside as the orchestra started to play. A waltz. Hell, yes, he knew how, he had practiced for hours, Parker showing him all the steps. Part of the plan, Miss Meredith.

"I'm surprised" she said as he spun her around.

"Surprised? Just wait, there's more on the way" he whispered in her ear. She paid no attention, smiling at the crowd as they applauded, a princess in the midst of her entourage.

When the music ended they stood at the edge of the dance floor. Dee bowed. She did not. Instead, she motioned to the corner of the room, to a couple of coeds standing near the cardboard box.

"He can dance, but that's about all" she said to the crowd.

A ripple of applause then, from the rest of her sorority, as the coeds in the corner opened the box and brought a silver plated dumb bell to her.

"As he would put it, this here's Phillip Dee" she announced, mimicking the country voice he had been speaking in. "And here's his prize, for being the dumbest man on campus. A dumb bell."

She handed him the dumb bell and stepped back. Waiting for applause.

Dee bowed again, stepped forward and shoved the dumb bell in her arms, standing beside her with an arm around her waist.

Posing for the camera as Rudy, the photographer from the paper, stepped from behind the bar and fired a flash bulb. With Dee smiling and Meredith shrieking, her face showing signs of some horrible nightmare.

"What . . . what's going on?" she gasped.

"Read tomorrow's paper" Dee answered. "I'll see it's delivered to your doorstep."

Meredith looked around for help. Confused, along with the rest of the crowd. Dee walked away as the music started again. Nodding at Parker. Heading for the parking lot. Time to wrap it up with a two column headline.

A tea dance straight from hell, Miss Meredith. Wait until you see your picture in tomorrow's paper.

Dee looked at his watch as he parked behind the paper. Running late, damn it, no time to change on the way. Grab the clothes behind the rumble seat and change in the men's room. Get out of this moth-eaten tux and go to work. See how that picture of Queen Meredith turned out. Relax and gloat, damn right.

Or maybe not, not with the gang in the city room laughing when they saw him, not with someone saying look at Dee, he's been auditioning for the circus, not with Lulu standing up and bowing. And not with Buck stopping him in the hallway to the men's room, not laughing at all, just shaking his head and staring.

"What the hell do you have on?" Buck grumbled.

"It's a tuxedo, Buck, I've been to a dance."

"A dance, at three in the afternoon? Wearing that?"

"It's something I rented, I know, it doesn't fit too well, but. . ."

"You rented that? Where? How much?"

"A place off Congress Street, five dollars, look, I. . ."

"I'll look, all right. Five dollars, hell, I'll put everybody in a tux, bring a little class to this goddamn paper." Still shaking his head, Buck walked past him then, laughing, mumbling something about tuxedos. In the men's room, changing clothes, Dee started laughing, too. Class, damned right, that's what that dance was all about.

By the time he got to his desk, wearing a standard coat and tie, he could see the city room had calmed down. No more laughing. Phones ringing, typewriters clattering, everyone at work. Except for Lulu, who had gotten up from the ring, walked across the room and was standing now in front of him.

Dee paid no attention, looking at a note on his desk instead. The police chief called, said the note, he wants to see you at the precinct station right away, he sounded urgent. Marked twenty minutes ago. The chief himself, damn, what does he want? And what does she want?

"What you have on looks better" said Lulu.

"I know, I know, it was. . ."

"Come with me" she said. "I want to show you something."

"Lulu, I just got here, I have to. . ."

"The mail room, young man. Come with me."

Bossy. Another bossy woman. Another Meredith. No jewels, no fancy necklace, but bossy, just the same. What the hell. Dee shrugged his shoulders, got up, followed her to the mail room, and saw where she was pointing.

"There" she said. "That's where you get your mail, that's where I get mine."

"Fine, Lulu, so what?"

"This letter is addressed to you. It was in my box. It's yours."

"All right. That's it?"

"I want you to take care of this."

"Take care of what?"

"My box. Everyone tries to stick something in it."

Dee tried not to grin. What's with Lulu? Those headlines she writes, and now this talk about her box, hell, she must be as dumb as Meredith. Or the biggest tease this side of the Colorado River.

"Stick something in your box? Not me, lady, I wouldn't dare."

"I'll bet you wouldn't" said Lulu, smiling as she walked back to the ring.

Dee watched. That smile. That walk. Too much. Concentrate, he whispered to himself, looking at the letter Lulu handed him. From Martha Trembley, the old policeman's wife. Good, get your mind off Lulu, get back to work.

Before he could get to his desk Ashley stopped him, coming up the staircase from the printing room downstairs. With a crumpled sheet of newsprint in his hand. And a scowl on his face.

"You and Parker, what are you up to?" demanded Ashley, holding the sheet of paper in front of Dee. A print of the picture taken at the dance. Big, three columns wide, with Dee in his tuxedo and a nightmare look on Meredith's face. Great. A winner, worth every penny.

"Breaking news, Amos."

"Breaking news in the amusement section? My ass."

"Amos, listen, it's. . ."

"And this tux you're wearing in this picture, I heard you had that on when you came in. Damn it, Phil, stop it, stop clowning around with Parker." Ashley wadded the print of the picture and threw it in a wastebasket, shaking his head.

"Right, Amos, stop clowning around."

"The police beat, that's your job. The Blotter, not Parker's crap."

"The police beat, right, the chief called, he wants to see me."

"What about? That Trembley feature? That was two weeks ago."

"Screw him. Hell, Amos, I left out the part about crooked voting."

"It could be he's caught on. Be careful, Phil."

"Caught on? To what, where to rent a tuxedo?"

"No, damn it, the Blotter, what we're doing with East Austin."

Dee did not reply. No need to. Amos had walked back to his desk, still shaking his head. He was right. Stop clowning around, stop talking about that tux. This game with Meredith, that's over and done.

Get the tux back to that rental shop. Get Debbie's car back to her apartment. Find out what the chief wants, see why the note said it's urgent. Stop clowning around, get back to real work.

The letter from Trembley's wife, that could mean some real work, indeed. Dee read it carefully, several times, after he parked in front of the precinct station.

Thanks for the story about her husband. A reminder about the crooked voting in East Austin. A prayer, of sorts, that the chief of police might listen to a reporter. Right. Real work, for sure, trying to get the chief to listen.

He was standing in front of the desk sergeant when Dee walked in. Dressed, as always, like the good guy in a cops and robbers movie, wearing a uniform covered with badges and medals.

Someday he'd be worth a full description, if Dee could work it in. Six feet four inches, armed with a pearl-handled forty-four he had never unholstered. The mayor's front man. A twenty one carat toady.

Dee could feel himself tightening up when the chief turned around and saw him. Edgy. Maybe a let-down after finishing off with Meredith. Or Buck and Amos on his butt about that damned tuxedo. Or maybe that letter from Trembley's wife.

Whatever, he could feel it. Something close to hostile, the way this chief was looking at him, like he was ready to spank him for being a bad boy. Bad boy, damned right, if he finds out what Trembley said is true.

"The kid reporter" said the chief. "Come over here, I have a question."

"A question? That's all? I was told it was urgent."

"No, I've been away. I just now read that crap you wrote about Trembley."

"So what's your question? If I'm going to write some more about him?"

The chief was silent for a moment, looking a bit uneasy. To hell with him. "Maybe I will" Dee added. "Things I left out the first time."

"That's what I wanted to see you about" said the chief.

"Really? What he told me, you're worried about it?"

"What he told you? He's senile, he's too old to know a damned thing."

"So what if he's old? What he told me, that 's not old, that's news."

"I'll give you some advice you'd better take, kid. Forget whatever Trembley told you." The chief towered over him, looking down as he spoke. Then back to the desk sergeant, as if that should end it.

"No" said Dee, loud, so the chief would turn around "No way."

"I told you" said the chief. "He's doesn't know a damned thing."

"That's why you won't listen to him? If you won't, I will."

"You're on thin ice, kid. I'm telling you, forget whatever you heard."

"Thin ice? Not me. You may be the one on thin ice, chief."

The chief stared at Dee, with a look on his face that seemed to say don't screw with me. Dee stared back, saying nothing. Without another word he walked out of the station, muttering to himself. To hell with the chief, he has business to take care of.

Still edgy when he got to the rental shop, Dee was starting to wonder. Damn it, what was bothering him? He could feel it. Tense, not even laughing as the clerk with the nametag Joe looked for the deposit on his tux, speaking with a Chinese accent.

"Wearing this" said the clerk. "You should have a picture."

"A picture? I have one, Joe, a nice one."

"A picture, yes, that would be nice. Good advertising."

"I'll send you a copy. Good advertising, right."

"Four dollars, the deposit. You come again."

"Four, good, but don't hold your breath, Joe."

Four dollars. Enough, just barely, for the last bit of business to take care of. A cab to follow him to Debbie's place, so he could drop her car off. Part of the plan, all worked out, all going well, even if he still felt uneasy about something.

One good thing, at least. No one is home at her apartment, he can leave her car in the parking lot and not face Debbie. No need to tell her what he used it for, she can guess when she reads the paper.

The taxi driver could not guess. A young man, college age, wearing horned rim glasses. Pushing a pile of books aside so Dee can get in the front seat of the cab. Looking hard at Dee and seeming puzzled.

"That there clunker, that ain't yours?" asked the driver.

"Not mine" said Dee. "I borrowed it for a tea dance."

"I ain't ever been to that, but square dances, I been to them."

"Head for Sixth and Congress" said Dee. "Where are you from?"

"Tyler, where they grow them roses. Up in East Texas."

"East Texas, right. So what are all these books for?"

"Gettin' ready to go to the school. I got to study to git in."

"School. You're driving a cab so you can. . ."

"I got a paper route, too. You ever have a paper route?"

"Once, sort of" said Dee, leaning back and starting to laugh. Watching the meter running as they turned onto Congress. Feeling better, much better now, even as the meter hit three dollars when they stopped at Sixth Street.

"The way you been laughin' you must like ridin' in cabs" said the driver.

What's that?" Dee replied, starting to calculate how much cash he had left now.

"I said you must like being in a cab" the driver answered.

"Sometimes" said Dee. "Sometimes it's good for the soul."

"Good for the sole? You got problems with your shoes?"

"No problems at all. Here's four dollars. Take it, you earned it."

"Well, dad gum, that's sure nice" said the driver, shifting gears and moving on.

Dad gum it is, said Dee to himself as he walked up the hill to the paper, still laughing. Dad gum, you bet, how do you like them apples, Miss Meredith, now there's two of us could've brung you to that dance.

"Lone Star draft, on my tab" said Dee when he reached the Split Rail Sunday afternoon.

"You don't have a tab" said the bartender.

"Too bad, because I'm broke, pal" said Dee.

"Then I'll lend you five bucks, Phil. Until payday, as always."

"And as always I'll have to pay you back six. That's usury, but what the hell."

"Not usury, Phil. Capitalism. Not like this crap your friend dropped off."

The bartender reached in a trashcan and came up with a crumpled poster. Not big, but printed in big red letters, calling for a mass protest in East Austin before next month's elections. With a signature at the bottom. Ashley's friend, Abe Liebwitz.

"I'll keep it" said Dee. "Something to look into."

"That's Commie shit, Phil. You know what the Communists stand for."

"Free love, the last I heard. Not a bad idea."

"No, damn it, they want to run everything, they. . ."

"Right, make everybody drink the same kind of beer. Lone Star."

Dee yawned, looking around, while the bartender went on ranting. Fine, take the five dollars, he's had a good night's sleep, with Galloway out of town and Parker not even coming home, it's time to relax, not argue about the Commies.

He wandered away from the bar, holding his beer in one hand and the poster in the other, searching for an empty table. Past a middle-aged couple looking at the picture in the paper, the lady starting to laugh a second or so after he sat down.

No wonder. Someone had reached over his shoulder and there it was. Shiny, just as it was in the paper, in the picture the couple had been looking at. Meredith's silver plated dumb bell, sure as hell.

The dumb bell. Plus a voice he recognized without looking up. Julie Trenton, Parker's dress shop lady friend. The one who tipped him off about Meredith. And maybe, just maybe, the reason why Parker never came home last night.

"Steve, I found him" said Julie. "Over here, he's all alone."

"He usually is" said Parker. "I can teach him to waltz, but that's about it."

"This thing is heavy, five pounds, at least" said Julie, pointing to the dumb bell.

"Julie picked it up after I left the dance" said Parker.

"On the lawn" said Julie. "After Meredith hurled it through a window."

"She's after your ass, Phil. Julie says Meredith called her lawyer."

"Well, hell" said Dee. "Sit down, have a beer, let's celebrate."

"We can't" said Julie. "We're in a hurry. Aren't we, Steve? In a hurry?" Grinning as she walked away with Parker, holding hands and whispering something in his ear. So Parker can only teach him how to waltz? Maybe one of these days. . .

"Five dollars for that" said the bartender, interrupting his thoughts, sitting down and pointing to the dumb bell. "Five dollars and we'll call it even, Phil. What do you say? I can use it to beat off drunks."

"And Commies, too. What do I say? I say bring me another beer."

Right. Maybe one of these days. See if Parker can give him a lesson or two. In something more than how to waltz.

Early Monday morning Dee was at his desk, waiting. Looking around the city room, nearly empty, with only a couple of reporters at work. Looking one more time at the Sunday edition. At Parker's review, The High And The Mighty. At the picture next to it, with the headline he'd smiled at again and again.

Dumb Belles Award
Goes to UT Sorority

No names in the story, only his own name in the cutline under the picture, presenting the Dumb Belle award to the president of a local sorority. Perfect, him smiling, a look on her face straight out of a drive in horror movie. No mention of her name, or even the name of the sorority. Only Parker's stab at satire.

Dee spread the paper on his desk, starting to clip the picture and the story with a pair of scissors, when he heard a voice and looked up. Buck, standing behind him, with his hands on his hips, looking down at the picture and grinning.

"You're here early, Phil. You figure she'll show up, is that it?"

"I'm betting on it. She'll be here, all right, raising hell."

"Who is she? I know, she's a sorority dame, but what's her name?"

"Meredith Ogletree. The name's not in the story, there's no chance of libel."

"Ogletree? That rich bastard from Fort Worth, Charlie's golfing partner?"

"Charlie Black? You're kidding Buck, don't tell me that."

"He won't know, he's out of town. Have a cigar."

"Black's golfing partner, damn. What's the cigar for?"

"I hate sororities. My wife was in one. If this babe shows up, send her to me, I want to meet her."

Dee went to the city room coffee pot, found a paper cup, and came back to his desk, looking at the picture. Cursing himself beneath his breath. Ogletree, the publisher's golfing buddy, damn, how could he have been so stupid, not checking to see who he was dealing with?

He did not have long to wait. Before he could drink the coffee he was dealing with her lawyer. A big bastard, looking down and telling him that's who he was, her lawyer. While Meredith stood behind him, staring at Dee, her eyes like daggers.

"She's here to see the publisher" said the lawyer. "He's a friend of her father."

"I know, Charlie Black. You can tell your client he's out of town."

"Who's next in command, or whatever you call it on a paper?"

"Buck Hooper, the managing editor, down the hallway."

"I will see him alone" said Meredith, walking away, leaving her lawyer standing in front of Dee. Telling him his name was Leonard Leland, he knew there were no grounds for legal action, but there were two other options.

"One, I can beat the shit out of you. That's what she really wants."

"Not good. What's my other option?"

"You can smoke this cigar. She's a pain in the ass, believe me."

Dee went to the coffee pot and brought back a cup for the lawyer. Who went on and on about his client, saying Ogletree had hired him to look out for Meredith, but don't worry about her father, he can't stand her, either.

Evidently Buck could stand her. Or at least could act like it. When she returned she smiled at her lawyer, and then looked down at Dee, not smiling at all. With her hands on her hips, still a princess, arrogant, master of her world. With a look on her face that spelled revenge.

"You're a fraud" she said. "You don't deliver papers."

"A frog, did you say? Speak up, lady, you're stuttering."

"You will be punished. Mister Buck has guaranteed it."

"What? No more tea dances with the Gamma Gammas?"

"He's going to make you ride around with police now. See how you like that."

She marched away. Prancing, in her high heels, with all her jewelry. A princess, not be to toyed with, by God. With her lawyer behind her, looking back at Dee and shrugging his shoulders.

Dee looked again at the picture, the two of them together. Him smiling, her shrieking. Meredith, still a Dumb Belle, by God. Buck had proven that just now, telling her how he'd be punished.

Two cigars. Not bad. And, my, my, now he has to ride around with police at night. Smoking cigars. Better than dancing with a bitch like her.

GENDARMES

Ashley looked at the poster from the Split Rail, then up at Dee, then back to the poster. Reading out loud. "Wake up, East Austin, this coming election will not be democratic." Staring at the initials at the bottom of the poster.

"A.L." said Dee. "You know what that means. Your buddy Liebwitz."

"The Split Rail. Celebrating, were you?"

"Celebrating? No, I was. . ."

"That Dumb Belle crap you wrote. Garbage. That's not reporting."

Ashley tossed the poster in a waste basket. Grumbling "Abe, so he's still in town. It's one damned thing after another." Dee waited, puzzled at the ugly look on Ashley's face, then reached in the basket for the poster and stuck it in a pocket.

"Amos, listen, whatever's eating you, I've got a hunch about this poster."

"Abe, he's calling for a protest before next month's elections. So?"

"Trembley says there's crooked voting in East Austin, right?"

"And you think Abe's found out something?"

"The police, they tore down Bubba's door, right?"

"You think this poster's tied to that? That's your hunch?"

Dee nodded, while Ashley looked for a telephone number, dialing the number, holding the phone across his desk so Dee could hear it ringing. Waiting, glancing at the poster. Putting the phone down when no one answered.

"That's the number he gave me. A boarding house some place."

"Amos, think. The elections, they're not far off, they're. . ."

"Late October. Six weeks away. So what?"

"There's time to track on this poster, find out where he had it printed."

"So you think you could find him, do you?"

"Right. Find out what he knows about the election in East Austin."

Dee waited, smiling. Hell yes, it's Sherlock Holmes time. Smiling until Ashley shook his head again. And said a hunch is not enough, let's see Buck, let's see how he wants to cover the election.

Fine, go see him. But halfway down the hall they stopped, Ashley pushing Dee aside, seeing who was coming from the managing editor's office. Charlie Black, the owner, the publisher, with a box in his hand. A box of chocolate nuggets.

"Hole in one" said Black. "Hold out your hands, have one."

Ashley nodded and held out his hand.

So did Dee, with his eyes on Black. Up close, the first time he'd seen what he really looks like. Tall, sun tanned face, middle aged, wearing a million dollar suit. Never around, always off somewhere playing golf. And walking past them now, to the city room, passing out chocolate nuggets.

"Don't eat that shit" said Buck when they entered his office. "Bad for the teeth. Chew on that and you'll need to see a dentist."

"A dentist? Amos has a friend who's a dentist, that's why. . ."

"To hell with dentists. Here, take this twenty, before I change my mind."

"A twenty dollar bill? What's that, some kind of severance pay?"

"Black read that Dumb Belle story, he said give you a bonus."

"A bonus, Buck? He didn't even recognize me in the hallway."

"Recognize you? Hell, he wouldn't know you from his caddy."

"But that picture . . . that's Ogletree's daughter . . . you said. . ."

"Turns out he despises her, hell, no wonder, that's why he. . ."

"Buck, we need to talk about this poster" said Ashley.

"No, you need to listen" said Buck, looking at the poster, handing it back to Ashley, reading a note on his desk, getting up, looking out a window with his back turned, cursing, turning around, looking at the note again, standing in front of them.

"You two, what did Black say in the hallway just now?"

"Hole in one, that's all" Ashley answered.

"Golf. Damn it, he should stick to golf. I don't get it."

"You don't get what?" asked Ashley.

"This note from Black. Read it, Amos. See if you can figure it out."

Ashley read the note, with Dee standing behind him, looking over his shoulder. Instructions to the managing editor. Black, saying he will handle the coming election himself, from now on the paper is not to print a word about it without his permission.

With a P.S. at the bottom of the note, pointing out the paper's policy, we do not report what happens in East Austin, any news from there worth printing he will handle that, as well.

"Damn" said Ashley. "He wouldn't tell you why?"

"Why? Because someone called him, Amos."

"Someone? Who? What did they tell him?"

"Whoever it was, they told him something he didn't like. So..."

"Someone called him?" Dee blurted out. "Maybe the police chief?"

Buck sat down, with a hard look on his face. Waiting for a moment, reading the note again when Ashley handed it back. Staring at Dee. Looking disgusted. Sounding angry as he spoke.

"All right, Phil. What do you know about this?"

"Nothing, Buck, not really, just a hunch, just. . ."

"Nothing. Then shut up. That twenty, take Lulu out to lunch."

"Lulu? Buck, listen. . ."

"Hell yes, she thinks you're cute. She must be blind as well as dumb."

With that Buck pointed to the door, saying get out, go back to work, he needs to think. Grumbling about Black, he's never stuck his nose in the news side of things before, all he cares about is making money and playing golf. . .

Dee could hear him grumbling still as Ashley closed the door and started down the hallway to his desk. Looking around the city room, making sure Black was gone, looking at the poster when Dee pulled it from his pocket.

"Amos, this poster, it. . ."

"To hell with Black. To hell with this election."

"You want me to track on this poster or not?"

"Buck hurt your feelings, did he?"

"What? Sure, I'm tired of him chewing me out, but. . ."

"He gave you that twenty, didn't he? Grow up, get your head straight."

Dee stood there, in front of Ashley's desk, waiting, saying nothing as Ashley sat down and leaned back with his eyes closed. With his mind on something else, it looked like. In a damned strange mood, for sure.

"All right, Amos. So what do you want me to do with this poster?"

"That poster? What about it?"

"What I said before, how it's all tied together, Abe, Bubba. . ."

"That hunch you had. No more hunches, damn it."

"Amos, listen, what Trembley said about crooked voting, that could be why. . ."

"You heard me. And no more crap like that Dumb Belle story."

"Okay, so that was crap, but this. . ."

"No more hunches. Stick to the Blotter, that's your job."

"The Blotter . . . the police beat . . . right. . ."

"Start acting like a real reporter for a change."

Ashley turned in his chair, with his back to Dee. Meaning that was the end of it. Leaving Dee to chew on what he'd said. No more hunches. Grow up. Start acting like a real reporter for a change.

Dee went to his desk and put the poster away. Looking at the twenty dollar bill from Buck. Enough for books next semester. Books, hell. Buck giving him a hard time, and now Ashley as well, enough for a bus ticket out of town. Sooner or later, damn it.

Sooner or later, right. Sooner or later.

"You're wrong about the chief" said the desk sergeant at the station, standing back as Dee thumbed through the precinct's list of the latest crimes and misdemeanors. Seeing nothing worth reporting. Saying nothing in reply.

"I heard what you yelled at him about Trembley" said the sergeant. Dee went on reading, keeping his mouth shut.

"The chief knows all about Trembley" said the sergeant. "I heard him say so." Dee remained silent, still keeping his mouth shut.

"But he couldn't tell you, Dee. He takes his orders from the mayor."

The mayor. To hell with keeping his mouth shut. Dee pushed the book away and looked the desk sergeant straight in the face.

"The mayor. Sergeant, what do you know about the mayor?"

"The mayor? Little Bob? He's a prick, stay away from him."

No point in asking what the chief might have told the mayor, or if the mayor might have been the someone who called Black. Or what the sergeant might have heard about the elections in East Austin. Do what Ashley said. No more hunches.

"Fine, so he's a prick. What else is new?"

"The two you're going with tonight, that's something new" said the sergeant. "Both ex-Marines, Barbour and Abrams. Around here, we know what the initials stand for. BA. For Bad Ass. Be careful what you write about them, Dee."

Be careful, right. Three months of The Blotter, being careful what he writes about East Austin, and still no clue about the cops who broke into Bubba's. And Trembley, being careful what he wrote about him, no telling what the chief might have told the mayor about that. So now be careful about two more cops? Right.

He waited, watching two policemen enter the station, with a young, pimply faced woman in handcuffs. Telling the desk sergeant to book her for driving a stolen car. The license plate was on the list to look for, the car had been impounded, and the sergeant could take it from there, maybe he could calm her down.

Dee saw their nameplates as they stood away from the woman. Barbour and Abrams. Trim, same height, same tough look on their faces. Both in their thirties. Loaded for bear, with side arms and billie clubs hanging from their belts. Looking hard at Dee when the desk sergeant told them he'd be tagging along tonight.

"Why us?" asked Barbour.

"Captain's orders" said the desk sergeant. "Public relations."

"Fuck the captain" said Abrams.

"Dee's just working his way through school" said the sergeant. "Go easy on him."

"Dee, that's your name?" asked Barbour. "All right, sit in the back seat, keep quiet and stay out of our way." He followed to their patrol car and got in, trying to get his mind off Buck and Ashley. Registration tomorrow for the Fall semester. Think about that. What courses to take.

A couple of history classes, not a bad idea, easy to pass by writing essays. One more year to graduate, and then get away. Away from all this crap he's gotten tangled up in. Black, the mayor, the chief of police, crooked voting in East Austin. Cops like Barbour and Abrams. Like Bordon and Jay. Get away from it all.

"So you're working your way through school" asked Barbour, looking back at Dee.

"Trying to" Dee answered.

"Really? Tell me something you learned" said Abrams, shifting gears.

"A French word" said Dee. "What they call police. Gendarmes."

"No shit" said Abrams. "The Japs, you know what they call reporters?"

"Assholes" said Barbour. "That's what they call reporters."

"Assholes" said Abrams. "Newspaper pricks, nothing but parasites."

"Turning out shit to entertain the public" said Barbour.

"We're talking about you" said Abrams over his shoulder.

"So what do you have to say to that? Speak up!" Barbour ordered.

"No way" Dee replied. "You said keep quiet, that's what I'm doing."

Quiet, but listening as Barbour went back to work. Talking on the radio, saying they were headed North, following a car with a tail light missing, any minute they would drop a fine on the driver, another forty dollars the mayor can stick in his pocket. Leaving Dee alone for now.

Parasites, their word for newspapermen. Not public servants like them. Dee grunted. For him, a way to get through college. About newspapers, hell, they could be right. Comic pages, horoscopes, football scores, junk, most of it. Dee and all the rest of them, parasites? Turning out shit for the public? Maybe.

No time for second thoughts right now. Barbour was on the radio, saying State 29, Roger that, we're on the way, call for an ambulance. Reaching through the window, setting the police light on top the car roof. With Abrams speeding up, the siren full blast, heading North, dodging traffic on a two lane highway.

Bad, Dee could tell by the voices on the radio. Something to write about, perhaps. Something to entertain the public.

It was worse than bad. Gruesome. A head on collision, he could see before they got there. Not yet dark, sunlight shining on two autos smashed together. On the other side of the crash three or four cars had stopped. A half dozen people had gotten out, staring at the bodies in the wreckage.

"Get away, get the hell away" shouted Barbour as he leaped out.

"Goddamn vultures" yelled Abrams behind him.

"Grab some flares, keep these bastards away" said Barbour.

Dee followed. No need for a doctor, he could tell at once. In one of the cars, a grey haired women, mangled, her head against a shattered windshield, her body twisted, dripping blood. Dead. With am arm hanging out the side of the car, her wristwatch unbroken. An odd looking watch with a red and blue face, still ticking.

In the other car a man, no doubt dead as well, his head mashed against the steering wheel. Both doors ripped away in the crash, hanging loose on the highway. On the floorboard of the car, next to the driver, a pack of Lucky Strikes. And an empty whisky bottle next to the cigarettes.

Dee walked away. Past the people hovering around the bodies. Past Barbour, yelling get away. Past Abrams, laying flares on both sides of the wreckage, telling the drivers of the other cars to turn around, take the detour one mile back. Past all that, to a ditch on the roadside, vomiting when he got there.

After a moment or so he stood up straight, wiped his mouth with a handkerchief, and walked back to the wreckage. Taking a deep breath. Facing up to his job as a reporter. Noting the details. How the cars collided. How the two policemen ordered the people from the other cars to back away.

And something else. The woman's arm hanging from the car. The wristwatch he had seen before was gone.

Dee looked around. Quiet now, only the sound of Barbour talking on the patrol car radio. Calm, saying tell the ambulance to turn the siren off, there's no need for that, all D.O.A, one women, one man, drunk driving it looks like, send a couple of tow trucks, we'll stick around.

D.O.A. Dead on arrival. Dee watched as the ambulance arrived. Two men got out, wearing gloves and plastic coveralls, opened the rear doors, and started unloading stretchers. Taking orders from Abrams. Pulling the bodies from the wreckage, laying them on the stretchers, covering both with white sheets head to toe.

"Wait" said Abrams. "The man, let me see his wallet. We'll need I.D."

"What about the woman?" asked one of the men from the ambulance.

"I'll look in her purse" said Abrams.

He did. Glancing at her driver's license. Writing her name and age on a clipboard. Along with the name and age of the man. Tossing the wallet and the purse on the stretchers. Laying the clipboard on the front seat of the patrol car. Watching the two men load the ambulance, close the doors, back away and head for Austin.

"You look pale" said Abrams. "First time you've seen this kind of shit?"

"First time" said Dee.

"You'll get used to it" said Barbour. "We did, you will, too."

"I don't think so" said Dee. "But I've got a question, maybe you can tell me."

"Drunk driving, if that's what you're wondering about" said Barbour.

"Not that" said Dee. "That wallet, that purse, what happens to them?"

"Don't worry about it" said Barbour. "They'll take care of it."

"Really? Like that woman's watch somebody stole?"

"First time he's seen a head on" said Adams. "He's imaging things."

"Keep your mouth shut" said Barbour. "Imaging things can yet you in trouble.".

Dee got in the patrol car, copied the names of the dead from the clipboard, and waited. While the tow trucks hauled the wreckage away, while Barbour and Abrams kicked the burnt out flares into a ditch.

Imaging things? No way. A missing watch, and he'd bet there's no money in that wallet or the purse when the ambulance reaches the morgue. Two crooked cops, in on the take, sure as hell.

Crooked. And hard as nails, just as the desk sergeant said, maybe harder, the way they acted at the crash scene, the way they talked as Abrams got in the driver's seat and headed back to Austin.

Barbour, asking Abrams how many drunk driving wrecks they had seen.

Abrams, answering over fifty now.

Barbour, saying it's always the same, it always reminds him of that Roy Acuff song. And starting to sing.

"What did you say it was brother? Who was it fell by the way? When whisky and blood run together, did you hear anyone pray?"

"You can't sing worth a damn" said Abrams.

"You know the rest" said Barbour. "See if you can sing any better."

"Hell yes" said Abrams. "I didn't hear nobody pray, dear brother, I didn't hear nobody pray, I heard the crash on the highway, but I didn't hear nobody pray."

"We need a guitar" said Barbour.

"Guitar, hell, what we need is something to eat."

"Not barbecue. Too early for East Austin."

"Later. Right now, let's see if Gertie's place is open."

Dee leaned back, hearing the words of the song again and again. When whisky and blood run together, did you hear anyone pray? The image of the bodies too. An ugly night to ride with cops. And all these two could think about was something to eat.

He stayed in the car when they parked in front of Gertie's Cafe. Hearing them bang on the door until someone let them in. Too early for East Austin, not time yet for barbecue? The two who broke into Bubba's, mean looking, Bubba's son in law had said. So go in, hit them with a question about that, see what they might admit to.

Dee got out and went to the door. Locked. With a sign saying Closed. Through a window he could see the place was empty. No sign of Barbour and Abrams. Odd. No answer when he knocked on the door. When he knocked again and an old, heavy set woman wearing an apron finally opened it.

"We're closed" she said. "Can't you read the sign?"

"The two policemen who just came in, where are they?"

"They're in the men's room. Go away."

"I'm with them. If you're closed, why did you let them in?"

"They're cops, that's why."

She stepped aside, mumbling she might as well let him in if he's with them. Dee followed her into the café, looking around, watching as she went to the counter and lifted the cover off an apple pie.

"I guess you want some too" she said.

"So they're cops" said Dee. "Why are you're afraid of them?"

"You want some pie or not?"

"What is it, you're afraid they'd break down your door?"

"You're not a cop, stop bothering me with questions."

"I'm a reporter, I'd like to know."

"A reporter, that's even worse."

"Gertie, bring some coffee, too" he heard Barbour say. Dee turned around and saw him coming from the men's room with Abrams. Sitting down at a table, waiting for her to serve them. Looking up at Dee.

"Go lie down in the car, take a nap" said Abrams.

"He should use the men's room first" said Barbour.

"Right, he looks like he peed in his pants" said Abrams.

"Bodies, that car wreck did him in" said Barbour.

"Poor baby, he should have been with us on Okinawa" said Abrams.

Dee sat down at the table, watching them eat apple pie. Listening to them talking to each other. About him. Mean bastards, for sure. So be it. Time to prod them, see what they know about Bubba's.

"East Austin" said Dee. "You go over there for barbecue, do you?"

"We do" said Barbour. "You've got something on your mind, what is it?"

"You know a place on Rosewood? Bubba's, it's called."

"We've been there" said Abrams. "What about it?"

"A few months ago, two policemen tore down the door and broke Bubba's leg."

"Really" said Barbour. "How do you know that?"

"They broke his son in law's arm and tore his flag off the wall, you two, you know anything about that?"

Barbour looked up from his pie, nodding to Abrams. Both of them silent, staring at Dee, their faces, cold as ice. Dee waited. No answer to his question. Only a grunt from Abrams as he laid some dollar bills on the table.

"You must like to gamble" he said, looking at Dee.

"I've played some poker" Dee replied. "So what?"

"You're gambling we could tell you what happened there."

"At Bubba's, that's right. I'm betting you could."

"You lose, you get a broken jaw, no more questions then."

"Leave him alone" Barbour interrupted. "Remember what the captain said."

"I know, public relations" Abrams replied. "Fuck the captain."

Abrams left the dollar bills on the table. For the apple pie and coffee. He and Barbour got up, without another word, and headed for the patrol car. Dee followed. Knowing he had just been warned. Don't bet on finding out who broke into Bubba's.

He sat in the back seat, weighing the odds. Gambling with the printers late at night, five card stud in the basement, after the paper's gone to press, that's on thing. Playing around with a couple of hardnosed cops, asking questions, that's could be risky. Damned risky. Wondering if he should bail out and head for the office.

"Slow down" he heard Barbour say, before he could make up his mind.

"What do you see?" asked Abrams.

"That school we passed, there's a flashlight on the second floor."

Abrams stopped, turned off the patrol car lights, and parked beneath a clump of trees. Next to an elementary school, near downtown. Watching. Dark in all the windows. Then a faint sign of light on the second floor.

Barbour reached to the ceiling of the car, brought down a shotgun, checked to see it was loaded, and got out. With Abrams behind him, both of them moving quietly across a playground to the school.

Dee sat in the car and waited. Walking distance to the paper. He could play it safe and leave right now. Stay out of trouble, no more questions. Run off by a couple of crooked cops.

No way. He got out and followed. Past a swing, tripping against a seesaw in the dark. No sign of where Barbour and Abrams had gone. No sign of a light anymore in the windows. All quiet, a false alarm, it looked like.

And then, all at once, the sound of broken glass, Barbour yelling stop, a pistol shot, more pistol shots, and a shotgun blast. Flashlights going on. In the shadows, someone running away, around a corner of the building.

"I'll get him" yelled Abrams, running across the playground.

"This one, goddamn it" said Barbour. "Why did he shoot?"

Dee looked down where Barbour's flashlight was pointed. A body on the ground, a young boy with a pistol in his hand, his chest blown open, a bloody mess in the broken glass outside an open door to the building.

Dead. As dead as the man and the woman in the car wreck two hours ago. The flashlight still shining on the boy's body, Barbour saying nothing. Quiet. Only Abrams' voice, yelling as he came running from the playground.

"The other one got away" said Abrams. "This one, he's. . ."

"He's dead" said Barbour. "Call it in."

"Have you been hit?" asked Abrams, shining his light on Barbour' shoulder.

"Grazed" Barbour answered. "See what he had? A twenty two caliber pistol."

Dee looked down at the revolver. Saying nothing. Waiting, while Adams went back to the patrol car, turned the lights on, found a driveway around the playground, and drove to the side of the building. With the car lights on, Dee could see Barbour's face. Grim as he looked at the body.

"Nothing in there worth dying for" said Barbour.

"How old do you think?" asked Abrams. "Fourteen, fifteen, maybe?"

"A goddamn kid" said Barbour. "No ID, I looked in his pants already."

Dee walked away, peering in the open door to the building. Shadows, the car lights shining on a row of lockers in a hallway. Barbour was right. Nothing in there worth dying for. Or killing for, except in self defense.

And even that, maybe that wasn't worth it. As the ambulance arrived, with lights all over the place, Dee could see Barbour leaning against the patrol car, shaking his head, looking down at the shotgun in his hands.

Best not to tell him it must be false, what he claimed. What Abrams had also said. How you get used to it. Bodies. Not when it's a fifteen year old kid lying dead, with his life snuffed out for nothing.

"Damn" yelled the ambulance driver. "You're keeping us busy tonight."

"Busy" said Abrams. "Something for this prick to write about."

"You" said the driver, looking at Dee. "You're a nosy bastard, aren't you?"

"Just doing my job" he replied. "Same as you."

"After that wreck, you asked what happened to the wallet and the purse?"

"Tell him" said Abrams. "He'd bet you stole whatever they had."

"Fuck him" said the driver. "He can check with the morgue."

"He won't" said Abrams. "He's not much of a gambler, he only bets on sure things." Dee kept his mouth shut, watching the ambulance haul the body away. Looking at Barbour and Abrams. Turning and leaving. Back to the office on foot.

Sure things to bet on? Two cops, who may or may not be as tough as they act. Who may or may not know who broke into

Bubba's place. Who might have done it themselves. Nothing to be sure about at all. Nothing to bet on. Not yet.

"You look pale" said Ashley as Dee reached his desk. "Life's too much, is it?"

"Not life" he replied. "Death."

He placed a sheet of paper in his Underwood and started typing. Two segments for The Blotter. Short. Nothing about their threats in the first part. Not a word about what Barbour and Abrams said. Not a word about the way they acted at the crash scene. Save all that, nail them in the second part.

"Two Dead In Highway 29 Collision" said Ashley, reading the headline Dee had written for the first segment. "A man and a woman. You've got their names and ages, I see. Two dead, now you know what it's like."

"It gets worse" said Dee.

"So you've seen some bodies in a wreck. So what?"

"I've had enough of these two cops, that's what."

"The police you rode with tonight? What about them?"

"They're bastards, they may be the ones who went after Bubba."

Dee wrote the second segment, about the shotgun shooting, and handed it to Ashley. With the headline Officer Kills Teenage Burglar. Ashley read it, looked again at the first segment, about the car wreck, and handed the second one back to Dee.

"The wreck" he said. "I want to check on this woman."

"Diane Eastman, that's her name. I think they stole her watch."

"You think so, do you? I told you, no more hunches."

"Amos, listen, what I saw. . ."

"This one about the shooting, this won't do, the way you've written it."

"Why? Because I named those bastards, Barbour and Abrams?"

"No, because it's personal. You've let your feelings get in the way."

"In the way of what? Nailing Barbour with a murder?"

Ashley said move over, put a clean sheet of paper in Dee's Underwood and started rewriting the shotgun report. Muttering, over his shoulder, how a real reporter would handle it, handing the rewrite to Dee when he was finished.

"Eyewitness Account of Burglar Shooting" said Dee, reading the new headline.

"The Blotter has your byline, we'll lead off with this."

"Just what I saw, all in the first person, it's different, Amos, so what?"

"When there's a shooting, there's an official enquiry, Phil."

"I get it . . . so I'm a witness, they'll have to call me to testify."

"If it's Barbour you're after, that's how you do it. Not in the paper."

Ashley got up, tossed Dee's original shotgun segment in a wastebasket, and started back to his desk. With the car crash report and the eyewitness account in his hands, ready to add them to the Blotter. Then he stopped, turned around, and came back.

"About these two policemen, I told you, no more hunches."

"Amos, damn it, Barbour and Abrams, they. . ."

"They what? You think they might be Holmes and Watson?"

"No . . . not that . . . I don't know . . . maybe. . ."

"Holmes and Watson. Another one of your hunches."

"That was a tip from Hattie, Amos. . ."

"Hattie. You should get your crap together."

Dee reached in his desk as Amos walked away. The note from Hattie. Watch out for a couple of crooked cops, it said, they go by the names Holmes and Watson. No names like that in the police department roster. A ten dollar scarf from that dress shop for Hattie as her reward, but no Holmes and Watson.

And his own notes, attached to hers. A call to Bubba's son in law. Linus, no point in asking again for the names he saw on the police who broke down the door. But did he hear what they called each other? If he did, could it be they called themselves Holmes and Watson? No reply there, either, only Linus saying leave him alone.

Holmes and Watson. Barbour and Abrams. The threat of a broken jaw, or maybe worse, if he keeps poking around.

Three dead in one night, too much. He could feel his hands starting to shake as he put the notes back in his desk. First time he'd ever seen such blood and gore. And now Ashley is on him for what he tried to write. An ugly night, for sure.

Ugly, with more to come. Dee braced himself as Buck and Ashley approached his desk, Buck holding some copy in his hand and gritting his teeth, Ashley coming behind him and shaking his head.

"You wrote this?" asked Buck, holding the car wreck report in front of Dee.

"I did, yes, just what I saw" said Dee, standing up.

"Diane Eastman" said Buck. "That name didn't ring a bell?"

"No . . . look. . ." Dee answered, "Her body, it was. . ."

"I checked" said Ashley. "Her husband's been notified."

"Front page" said Buck, turning to Ashley.

"I'll write it" said Ashley. "With a picture of the Eastmans together."

"Good" said Buck. "But don't mention that book they wrote on Johnson."

"I understand" said Ashley. "Not a word about Landslide Lyndon."

"Not a word" said Buck. "It makes Senator Johnson look like a crook."

Dee sat down, gripping the edge of his desk. That book the Eastmans wrote. How the bosses in Duvall County made him a Senator when they counted the votes again. Just barely, but enough to win the whole damned state. The Democratic primary, same as being elected, with no Republicans in Texas, and the Supreme Court wouldn't touch it.

The Eastmans, two professors, married, damn it, he had read their book, how could he miss that name?

"The car wreck bit, that goes in the Blotter" said Ashley. "I'll do the rest."

"Damn it, Phil, you should have known who she was" said Buck.

"His mind was on the cops he was riding with" said Ashley

"The cops? What about them?"

"He thinks they're are after him for nosing around."

"Hell, yes" said Buck. "In Duvall county they shot a reporter for nosing around."

Buck was grinning as he looked down at Dee. Okay, so they murdered a reporter, from San Antonio or someplace. For digging into that election recount. Another Texas legend, another unsolved crime. So, damn it, why was Buck grinning about it?

"So we get a dead reporter" said Buck. "That's good for circulation."

"Buck, listen, don't joke about it" said Dee.

"Joke, hell, you remember where you rented that tuxedo?"

"That tux? Damn it, we're talking about a murder, we're. . ."

"Go back, use that twenty, see if they can sell you a bullet proof vest."

Buck was still grinning as he walked away. With Ashley behind him. Dee shook his head. To hell with them both, if they had been with Barbour and Abrams, they'd be the ones looking for bullet proof vests.

He leaned back in his chair, staring at his typewriter. Eastman, so he should have recognized the name. So take a course from her grieving husband, see what he knows about Duvall county. See what he knows about staying alive.

At two in the morning Dee held a glass in his hand. Empty again. Watching Galloway and Parker go through the final edition. Hearing Galloway grumble about a printing mistake in his column, hearing Parker murmur as he turned to the metro section and glanced at The Blotter.

"Damn" said Parker. "This eyewitness crap, you need another drink, Phil."

"Read the next part" said Galloway. "What he wrote about the car wreck."

"Two dead in a head on" said Parker. "Drunk driving."

"You know what they say" Galloway muttered. "If you don't drive, drink."

Parker reached for a bottle of Ancient Age, poured bourbon in Dee's glass, added ice cubes, and set the morning paper on the bar. Dee said nothing, looking down at The Blotter, shaking his head.

"It could be worse" said Galloway. "You could be coaching the Longhorns."

"Worse than that" said Parker. "You could be a Panda bear."

"The way they look, they'll be lucky to win half their games" said Galloway.

"A Panda bear? Steve, what the hell are you talking about?" asked Dee.

"They're biggest problem, no quarterback" said Galloway.

"Panda bears, that's what" said Parker. "Here, look at this."

Parker pushed the paper aside, reached under the bar and bought out a copy of *National Geographic*. With the pages ear-marked. An article about a zoo in China, with pictures, a half dozen pages of pictures. The Chinese, mating Panda bears for export.

"Sixty times in twenty four hours" said Parker. "Look at that Panda hump."

"Sixty times?" said Galloway. "Let me see that."

"Sixty times" said Parker. "That would be a fortune at Hattie's."

"But not in twenty four hours" said Galloway. "Three years at least."

"My next life, that's what I want to be" said Parker. "A Panda bear."

Dee pushed the magazine aside, reached for his drink, and downed half a glass of Ancient Age. All at once, swallowing hard, almost choking. Smiling as he looked at Galloway and Parker. Then breaking out in laughter.

"No way" he said. "You couldn't hack it as a Panda bear."

"Maybe not" said Parker. "But at least you're laughing now."

"Laughing, hell" said Dee. "I'm getting drunk. I may stay drunk from now on.."

"You can't" said Parker. "You have to register tomorrow."

"Damned right" said Galloway. "One more year, you're finished."

"You graduate, we'll bring the cheerleaders back" said Parker.

"Good idea" said Dee. "Let's hope I live that long."

"What are you worried about?" asked Galloway. "Dying of thirst?"

"Not that" said Dee. "Two cops who might do me in. If I don't nail them first."

GUARDIANS

Registration for the Fall semester. September, a warm and humid Texas morning, no breeze, no clouds, the sun beating down on six lines of students, moving slowly, step by step, to a row of tables on the sidewalk in front of Gregory Gym.

Where men in shirts and ties were sitting. Looking bored. As the students came to the tables, read through a list, signed a form and waited. For the men to rubber stamp a registration permit. Notary publics, with badges on their shirts to prove it.

Above each table a sign read Loyalty Oaths Required by Law, with part of the alphabet tacked on a poster beneath it. Students A-D Sign Here, said the poster on the table in front of Dee's line.

Edgy from the night before, from riding with Barbour and Abrams, from drinking to forget what he'd seen, he listened to the students around him grumbling. About the loyalty oaths, about standing in line before they could register for courses.

It's the Cold War, someone said. That's how you get guys like Joe McCarthy, raising hell about the Commies.

Cold War, my ass, said the fellow behind him, does this feel like cold? It must be a hundred and ten at least.

Every semester we have to do this, someone said, that's twice a year, three if you go to summer school, you'd think once is enough.

No, someone else said, you might join one of these subversive groups between semesters, that's why you have to keep on swearing you're not a member.

Member, hell, someone added, you can belong to anything you want, including the goddamn Communist Party, there's no law against it.

Sure, someone said, but if you admit it you can't go to school here, and if you lie about it they can get you for perjury.

That's right, someone said, they can get you for perjury, there's a warehouse where they keep this crap on file, that's how they get you.

Perjury, my butt, someone added, that sorority girl who got her picture in the paper, a Dumb Belle that reporter called her, they should get her for being just plain stupid.

Perjury, someone gasped, you're saying this list of subversive groups includes sororities now, is that what you're saying?

Ask that blonde at the table, said someone else, she's been going through the list for five minutes, she's the one who's holding us up.

"I know her" said Dee. "Debbie Decker. I'll talk to her, see if I can speed her up, save my place in line."

He walked to the table and whispered in her ear. "Debbie, it's Omar, don't worry about it, just sign the form, you're holding up the line."

"Go away" she said. "I'm in enough trouble already."

"Trouble? Sign it and wait for me, you hear?"

"I'm done. I'll wait on the steps, I'll show you."

Dee went back to the line, said she's signed it, we can move on, she wanted to be a cheerleader, she's a little slow, I'm afraid, she's worried about something.

Hell, someone said, maybe she's one of the Commie cheerleaders in the Ranger, if that's who she is no wonder she's worried.

Brilliant, that remark, like everything else he'd heard while standing in line. Commie cheerleaders? Who dreamed that up, the state attorney general? Loyalty oaths, big deal, get in and register for classes, that's what counts.

He glanced at the list when he got to the table, ran through it, from A to Z in twenty seconds, signed the form, and walked on to Debbie, waiting on the steps leading into the gym. Cleared for registration.

"Your name's not Omar" she said. "I saw your picture in the paper."

"Fine, it's Phil" he replied. "What's this about being in trouble?"

"The lady you gave that dumb bell to, she's your new girlfriend?"

"Forget her, damn it, what's this trouble you're in?"

"You haven't read The Ranger, Omar? I'm in it."

"That's it? I have two cops after me and you're worried about. . ."

"Here, I'll show you. This came out two days ago."

She sat down on the steps, opened her purse, and handed him a copy of the *Texas Ranger,* the monthly campus humor magazine. Always full of dirty jokes and innuendo. "Look on page fifteen" she said, sounding nervous.

No wonder. At the bottom of page 15, a picture of Debbie and her would be cheerleader friends, grinning and showing off. No doubt taken the night of the tryout, the same night Parker brought them home to clean the kitchen.

In the picture they were wearing the same flimsy costumes, but the color of their wigs had been changed from orange to bright red. And across the picture, a diagonal caption spelled out the magazine's stab at humor:

UT's Latest Lure, Commie Cheerleaders, Free Love, Anyone?

"That's what I mean" she said. "We're not Communists."

"You're not in trouble" said Dee. "It's only a joke."

"We're loyal, you have to be loyal to be a cheerleader."

"I'm sure you are, Debbie, it's nothing, forget it."

"Free love? What does that mean?"

"Communism, that's what folks believe they preach."

"There's no Commie cheerleaders in that list, I looked."

"I know. That free love business, Debbie, that's a joke, as well."

"Then we should have had a full page, like this woman here."

She turned the pages so he could see. He did, and smiled. A full page picture of Hattie, pink parasol and all, standing in front of her house. No way to know where they got the picture, but the joke was clear enough:

Texas Ranger Girl of the Month, Give Her A Ring

"Who is she?" Debbie asked. "They don't tell you her name."

"No need to" said Dee. "Her friends know who she is."

"What's so funny? Why are you laughing?" Debbie asked

"Hattie, there's no free love there" said Dee.

"It says give her a ring, you could give me a ring."

"Sunday, we'll go for a ride, I'll show you what free love means."

"No sir, you said that's Communism, I just signed that loyalty oath."

Debbie got up, patted Dee on the head, left her copy of the Ranger with him and went in the gym, bouncing her hips as she went up the steps. Dee watched and frowned. Too bad. Maybe some day he'd get lucky, but not with her, he'd have to explain free enterprise first. Forget it, that's what Hattie's place is for.

He followed, ready to register. A couple of history classes, one from Eastman for sure. Then head downtown. Smiling as he looked at the picture again. The Communist scare, that's one thing, naming Hattie girl of the month, that's real subversion.

He could hear them now, the politicians who run things. Her regular customers, whispering this can't be! It's worse than Communism! A picture of Hattie, this undermines public morals!

Dee was still smiling as he left the gym. What could they do about it? Besides wring their hands and whisper it's a scandal? Add the Ranger to that list of subversive groups?

Make everyone take an oath not to read it? Keep on whispering it's subversive?

No telling.

The mayor was not whispering. When he entered the precinct station, on his way to lunch, Dee heard him shouting. Little Bob

Macdill, standing in the middle of the room, short and fat, wearing his usual Stetson hat and cowboy boots, raising hell about something.

"Do it, damn it!" the mayor yelled, pointing his finger at the chief of police, who was standing next to a man Dee recognized at once. Meredith Ogletree's lawyer, Leonard Leland, shaking his head as the mayor went on yelling.

"What are they arguing about?" Dee asked the desk sergeant.

"That punk who runs the college magazine" the sergeant answered.

"The Ranger editor, you mean, what about him?"

"Little Bob wants the chief to throw him in jail."

"Arrest him? Put him in jail? Damn. . ."

"He can't, that lawyer blocked him."

"I'll stick around. This could be an item for the paper."

The sergeant reached under the counter for a copy of the paper, turning the pages to the metro section, glancing at The Blotter, at Dee's byline account of the shooting at the school three nights ago. He looked at Dee and grunted.

"The paper, I read it, what you wrote about Barbour."

"That boy he shot, just what I saw, that's all."

"Hell, from what I heard, Barbour thinks you did him a favor."

A favor? No time to ask how that could be, not with the mayor stomping past him, cursing, on his way out of the station, followed by the chief. And Ogletree's lawyer, Leland, coming behind them, puffing on a cigar.

"My, my, it's the young man who writes for the paper" said the lawyer.

"And you're Leland, right? What's this about the Ranger editor?"

"Hard to tell. Have you heard from Meredith lately?"

"No, I haven't, what does that mean, hard to tell?"

"The mayor wants him arrested, but he won't specify the charges."

"Charges? What charges? That picture of Hattie, that's not a crime."

"Whatever it is, he won't say. I had no trouble getting an injunction."

"You represent the Ranger, too? You're their lawyer?"

"The crap they print, they need a lawyer."

Dee followed Leland out of the station, to the parking lot in back. Not sure what to ask. An injunction, how long will that last? The mayor, what's Little Bob up to, if he won't say what he's ticked off about?

"Who knows?" Leland answered. "He's mad as hell about something."

"About the Ranger? You've blocked him, right? What can he do?"

"See his pals at the Capitol, maybe. That's my guess."

"The state legislature? What for? I don't get it."

"Money, Dee. They could cut off funds for publication."

"Keep the Ranger from being printed? On what grounds?"

"Grounds? Go watch, you'll be surprised how those idiots operate."

"The legislature, sure, I've watched a couple of times, but. . ."

"Keep your eyes on Meredith, she may surprise you, too."

Leland drove away, leaving Dee in the parking lot. Distracted. Keep his eyes on Meredith, why? And the desk sergeant, saying Barbour thinks he's done him a favor, how? To hell with that, go have lunch and get to work, write about this injunction.

"You're bothered, what is it now?" asked Ashley, when Dee got to the office two hours later, sat down at his desk, and started typing. Slow going. Leland was right, who knows what's eating Little Bob? An injunction, not much to write about.

"It's the mayor, Amos. He was at the precinct station, he. . ."

"The station, all right, go ahead, what did you hear?"

"There's a picture of Hattie in the Ranger, he's. . ."

"I know about the picture, what about Little Bob?"

"The Ranger editor, he tried to have him arrested, he. . ."

"Not enough. Come with me, Buck's waiting for us."

Not enough? Not enough for what? Dee followed Ashley to Buck's office, puzzled. More puzzled when he saw who was there. Galloway, sitting in a corner and shaking his head about something.

"Sit down, Phil" said Buck. "You have a job to do."

"He's not up to date" said Ashley. "He only knows about the Ranger."

"Little Bob" said Buck. "We're going to hang that bastard."

"Why?" asked Dee. "He's gone off the wall, but. . ."

"He's an asshole" said Buck. "We're going to nail him for corruption."

"This is Black's idea?" asked Dee. "This is about the election?"

"No, it's about the legislature" said Ashley. "They're meeting tonight."

Buck turned around in his swivel chair, looking at the Navy pictures on the wall. While they waited. Dee puzzled, Ashley patient, Galloway saying this has nothing to do with sports, shutting up as Buck spun around in his chair.

"It does" said Buck. "Tyrell's going to spill the beans."

"Tyrell, who's that?" asked Dee.

"Hopalong Tyrell, he plays halfback for the Longhorns" said Galloway.

"He's also a member of the legislature" said Ashley.

"They're meeting tonight" said Buck. "Little Bob's seen to that."

"To cut off funds for the Ranger magazine" said Ashley.

"I know" said Dee. "The lawyer I talked to, he said they. . ."

"They can't refuse" said Buck. "They're in too deep."

Buck leaned forward, spelling out what he'd heard. How the mayor had gotten to the legislature. Fixing parking tickets, hiring whores to entertain them, that sort of thing. So the legislature would bend over backwards, with special tax rates for the city, with money for jobs and buildings.

"Bribes, that's how this bastard keeps getting elected" said Buck.

"Fine" said Dee. "So why hasn't the paper exposed him before?"

No reply. Nothing but silence, Dee waiting for an answer, Galloway half asleep with his eyes closed, Buck looking over his shoulder at the Navy pictures, Ashley nodding, looking at Dee and finally speaking.

"Buck needs proof" said Ashley. "He thinks he'll get it tonight."

"This fellow Tyrell" said Buck. "I've had a tip he's fed up."

"He's on the ethics committee" said Ashley.

"Wait" said Dee. "There's something missing here."

He looked at Buck, shaking his head. That picture in the Ranger, sure, the local politicians would scream about it, even the ones in the Capitol. But the mayor, even if he's as crooked as Buck says, what's he worried about? What's so important about that picture of Hattie?

"Little Bob" said Dee. "Why's he so bothered about the Ranger?"

"Because he's an asshole" said Galloway. "An asshole Aggie."

"Who knows? Maybe you'll find out tonight" said Buck.

"Buck wants you to cover this meeting" said Ashley.

"Damn it, Buck" said Dee, "I don't know crap about the legislature."

"Amos, tell the AP guy to read him in" said Buck. "It's a crime, what's been going on, it goes with the police beat."

The police beat, right, keeping him busy enough already, looking for dishonest cops. The break in at Bubba's, the watch stolen from a dead professor, a kid murdered in cold blood, and now he has to cover the legislature too? Why? This corruption crap Buck's on to, what if it's only hearsay?

No point in arguing about, not with Buck pointing to the door. And grumbling, once again, watch out for sharks and the shore patrol.

"He's full of shit" said Galloway as they left the office.

"About the mayor, you mean. It could be only rumors, what he's heard."

"No, about Hopalong. Even if it's true, he wouldn't squeal."

"Tyrell, he plays football? What's he doing in the legislature?"

"He likes to make speeches. Last week a coach put tape around his mouth."

"To shut him up? Damn, so how'd he get elected?"

"Some little town near Lubbock. Out there he's famous."

"Why? Because he plays for the Longhorns?"

"No, because of the way he clowns around, hell, if he keeps it up, he'll be elected governor some day. He'd be perfect."

Galloway was laughing as he headed for the sports department. Leaving Dee at his desk, thumbing through a handbook on the legislature. The Texas Senate, the House of Representatives. All mish mash. In a moment Galloway came back, no longer laughing.

"The mayor" he said. "I don't know about tonight, but bag him if you can."

"That's what Buck wants" said Dee. "What do you have against the mayor?"

"He's an Aggie prick, Phil. He ruined my hat, that bastard."

"At Hattie's . . . sure . . . I remember now. . ."

Dee nodded. What had they told him about that night? The mayor, at Hattie's, saying the Aggies would stomp the Longhorns, crushing Galloway's hat, having his aide tear off Parker's sleeve, lying about it, saying it didn't happen there, he'd never been to Hattie's, it was in a bar downtown.

And now he's going after the Ranger, for some reason he won't admit to, either. The Ranger, lying about what happened at Hattie's, strange, maybe some way it's all connected. But how?

He leaned back in his chair, looking at the handbook. Hearing Ashley's voice behind him. Hearing him say it's the Navy, the war's been over ten long years and Buck's still thinking about the Navy.

"The Navy" Dee replied, turning around. "What's that have to do with Little Bob?"

"That pharmacist who served on Buck's ship, he just came to town, remember?"

"Sure, I met him, his wife, too, they moved because of all the noise, so what?"

"The mayor's hit him with a big-time license fee. That's why Buck's stepped in."

"A license fee? What about all this crooked shit he was talking about?"

"I wouldn't know. Just do your job, and remember what he likes to say."

"Right. Look out for sharks and the shore patrol."

Ashley walked away, leaving Dee to himself. Fine, the mayor has a bug up his ass about a picture in the Ranger, the managing editor has a bug up his ass about the mayor, and now he has to listen to a football player spilling the beans to the legislature. Because it goes with the police beat.

Spill the beans? What beans?

Twilight, with the sky barely dark, the spotlights were already on atop the state capitol, pointing to the Lone Star flag above the dome. Twenty feet taller than the national capitol in Washington, Dee mused as he walked up the steps and into the lobby, that's Texas for you, so big there's plenty of room for crooked politicians.

A half dozen were gathered in the lobby, armed with brief cases, talking in whispers, conferring, it looked like, beneath a painting of Sam Houston. Maybe crooked, maybe not. Dee walked on, past a statue of Davy Crocket, to the chambers where the House meets. Where Hopalong Tyrell would expose them all, if Buck was right.

"Sit down, Phil" said a middle aged man at the press table in the back of the House chambers. "They told me to give you a hand." An Associated Press reporter who had once worked for the paper. Until the AP lured him away to cover the state capitol.

"Which one is Tyrell?" asked Dee, watching the room start to fill, seeing thirty or forty members of the legislature wandering to their seats, hearing the Speaker of the House pound his gavel and announce this special session is in order.

"That's Tyrell, wearing the Longhorn jacket" said the AP man. "He loves to talk, when he sees that TV camera over there they won't be able to shut him up."

Dee listened as a man stood up and started to speak. One of the group he'd seen in the lobby. Reading a speech already written, denouncing the University for allowing smut, moving that the House refuse to fund the Texas Ranger any further.

Another man he'd seen in the lobby seconded the motion, someone shouted "Point of order!" and the Speaker pounded his gavel again, flipping through a notebook and reciting the rules for a special session. Dee could see Tyrell was smiling.

"Smut, that's the magic word" said the AP man. "That makes it a moral matter, so by rule the members of the ethics committee will have first crack, without interruption. We're in for a long night now, just as soon as Tyrell gets the floor."

He was right. Tyrell raised his arm, stood up when the Speaker nodded, and started talking. In a drawl, on and on, about something worse than smut, he said. Sandstorms. How sandstorms were ruining West Texas, leaving people lonely and unhappy.

Dee looked at his watch and shook his head. Sandstorms? What the hell did that have to do with Little Bob? With all the bribes Buck talked about? What was Tyrell up to? Getting ready to charge the mayor with paying someone to make the wind blow?

Not that. After twenty minutes or so Tyrell offered an amendment to the motion on the floor. Sandstorms are evil, he said. So whatever money comes from cutting off the Ranger, that money must be used to help the victims of sandstorms.

"Clever" said the AP man. "He knows these people won't give money to the victims of anything. And sure as hell not to someone in West Texas."

So what? Dee groaned, still wondering what Tyrell was up to, seeing he still had the floor. And was moving on to another amendment. Something about stealing cars. The state still has a law for hanging a horse thief, said Tyrell, it's right there in the books, it's time y'all pass a law for hanging car thieves, that's ethics, too.

Dee was not the only one who groaned. When Tyrell finished with his car thief amendment several members of the legislature shook their heads, looked at the clock on the wall, got up, and left. Dee looked also. Well past nine already.

"If this goes on much longer they won't have a quorum" said the AP man.

It went on. And on. Tyrell, starting to talk about sin now. Drawling big time. Y'all think the Ranger is sinful? Y'all oughta look around, sin is all over, this next amendment will outlaw sin, no more sin in Texas, y'all cain't turn this down.

Damn it, let's get this over, let's vote, yelled one of the men from the group in the lobby. Hell no, not yet, someone else yelled, let's hear more from Hopalong about sin, maybe he'll tell us about Hattie's.

"Y'all know about Hattie, I guess ya'll do" Tyrell smiled and answered in a loud voice. "Well, sir, if ya'll do, go ahead and vote, y'all cain't vote against this. Ya'll would be condonin' sin, yessiree Bob, that's what ya'll would be doin' all right."

"There won't be a vote" said the AP man. "There's not enough left."

He was right again. A moment later the Speaker banged his gavel, announced there is no longer a quorum, by rule the motion on the floor is dead, along with Mister Tyrell's amendments, this session is adjourned, God Bless the State of Texas.

"Two paragraphs" said the AP man. "I'll put it on the wire right away."

"Fine" said Dee. "An evening wasted. No point in my writing anything."

"Buck thought something big would break, did he?"

"He did. And he'll have my ass if I don't find out why it didn't happen."

Tyrell was alone, standing up, leaning against his desk, as Dee approached him. Not very big, built like a halfback, all right.

Looking like he could talk all night. Reaching in his jacket for something. A banana. Starting to peel it, holding it in front of Dee, with a smile on his face.

"Howdy" said Tyrell. "I know you. Want a bite?"

"No, look, I need to. . ."

"I saw you at that tea dance. How'd you learn to do the waltz that way?"

"You were there? Okay, but. . ."

"You did Meredith a big favor."

"Meredith, no, listen, I. . ."

"Some talent scout saw it, that goofy picture you printed. She's headed for Hollywood now, you didn't know that?"

Dee shook his head and stared at Tyrell. Chewing on that damned banana. What's he yakking about? Hollywood, what about Little Bob? All this crap about sandstorms and horse thieves and outlawing sin, what the hell was he up to?

"The mayor. . ." Dee started to say. "What do you. . ."

"The mayor? I never met him, what about him?"

"That picture in the Ranger, he's after the editor, he. . ."

"The Ranger editor? He's in my fraternity, what about him?"

"Bribes, I've heard the mayor is a crook, he uses bribes to. . ."

"They ain't gonna bribe me, no sirree, they cain't close the Ranger down. That editor's my friend."

Still smiling as he tossed the banana peel in a wastebasket. As he did it finally dawned on Dee, what Tyrell had been up to. Protecting a friend. Buck was wrong, sure as hell, Hopalong doesn't know a damn thing.

Or maybe he does.

"No siree, they cain't close it down. They gotta see that other picture."

"There's another one? Another picture? Who's in it?"

"You'll jus' have to wait and see. Yessiree Bob, you'll see."

Tyrell winked and walked away. Fast. Out of the House chambers before Dee could ask another question.

Wait and see? See what?

Dee waited a moment, wondering, and then walked out himself. Into the hallway. Where Leonard Leland was waiting. Meredith's lawyer. The Ranger's lawyer. Smoking a cigar.

"I was watching" said Leland. "Tyrell loves television."

"He mentioned another picture. You know anything about that?"

"Another picture? No, all I know is the Ranger's safe for now."

"Safe from Little Bob. I still don't get it, what he's after."

"Who knows? Keep your eyes on him. That's my advice."

"I don't know, I. . ."

"Keep your eyes on Meredith, too."

"I know, Tyrell told me. She's gone to Hollywood. Big deal."

"That picture in the paper, she looked so shocked they've cast her in a horror movie. They're shooting the damned thing already."

Leland was still talking as they walked through the lobby and out of the building. Saying it's mighty strange, what the mayor's up to, hell, some times I wonder if I even know which way the wind is blowing.

"You want a ride to the paper?" he asked. "I'm headed that way."

"No thanks" said Dee. "I'll walk. I need to think."

Think. Right. Try to add it up.

The two policemen, Abrams and Barbour, mean as hell, stealing that dead woman's watch, warning him to stop nosing around when he asked what they knew about the break in at Bubba's place in East Austin. . .

Black, passing out chocolate nuggets for a hole in one, telling Buck someone called him, he will handle the coming election himself, saying the paper's policy is firm, no reporting on what happens in East Austin. . .

Trembley, telling him there's crooked voting in East Austin, the police chief telling him Trembley's senile, Ashley's buddy Liebwitz printing a poster warning East Austin they're votes aren't democratic. . .

And Ashley, in a damned strange mood, telling him to grow up, get his act together, no more hunches, no more crap like that Dumb Belle story, start acting like a real reporter for a change. . .

Buck, sending him off on a wild good chase because of a Navy buddy. The desk sergeant, saying Barbour wanted to thank him. Meredith, in Hollywood because she screamed in a picture he set up. . .

The mayor, raising hell about Hattie's picture in the Ranger. Tyrell, talking the House to death because the Ranger editor is a fraternity brother. And then saying there's another picture on the way.

Odd, damned odd, all of it.

Walking back to the office he stopped on Congress Avenue and looked back at the Capitol. Maybe that's what it really means, watch out for sharks and the shore patrol. It means you can never tell what's going on around you.

He sure as hell couldn't.

Dee pulled a message off the spindle on his desk, read it, and grunted. Some reader had called in with a comment about the Blotter. But nothing from Buck. Not a single word about last night.

Nothing about Tyrell in his mail box, either. Only a statement from the bank. Twenty one dollars and forty cents, along with that bonus enough for textbooks for the Fall semester. And a second letter, local postmark, with no return address.

He started to open the envelope as he walked back to his desk, seeing Ashley coming down the hall. From Buck's office. Shaking his head. With a troubled look on his face. In a bad mood still. Not good, not good at all.

"Leave me alone" said Ashley.

"All right, I will . . . but Buck, what did he say about last night?"

"What did you expect? He thinks someone let him down."

"Not me, damn it. I covered Tyrell, like he told me to, I. . ."

"So you did. Now leave me alone."

"Who gave Buck that tip? That's who he should raise hell with."

"I wouldn't know. I don't know about the mayor, either."

"But why did he call that special session? That was his work, Amos."

"So what? Let Buck worry about him. That's not your job."

"Fine, but what does Little Bob have against the Ranger?"

"I don't know, and neither do you. Leave me alone."

"Okay, but why is he trying to close it down? That picture of Hattie, that's all? Amos, listen, I'm telling you, there's something rotten here."

Ashley muttered "Just do your job, goddamn it" and walked away. Cursing. Leaving Dee alone and wondering. What's been eating Amos? Buck, what exactly did he say about last night?

No telling. He tore open the envelope with no return address and looked inside. A short, handwritten note, scribbled on a page from a memo pad. He read it again and again. Shaking his head. So that's what the desk sergeant meant. When he said Barbour thinks you did him a favor. A favor, damn it.

Dee: The District Attorney read your eyewitness account of the shooting at the school and closed the books on that. A break for me.

Semper Fi. Sgt. Barbour.

A break for Barbour? Like hell. And Ashley, what did he say the night of the shooting? Keep your feelings out of it, write only what you saw, a kid with a pistol in his hand and then a shotgun blast, they'll call you to testify, that's how you do it if you have to, not in the paper.

Really? So what will he say now, when he sees this note from Barbour? Spin off another story about Duvall County, about the sheriff there, about a dead reporter murdered for nosing around? Mimic Buck and say go get a bulletproof vest? Or worse, say fine, get shot, raise the paper's circulation.

Ashley said nothing at all. Not a word when Dee laid Barbour's note in front of him. He looked at the note for a second or so, crumpled it into a wad, tossed in the waste basket next to his desk, stood up, reached for his coat and hat, and walked slowly to the elevator. In another moment he was gone. Out of the city room, without a word.

Dee watched as Ashley disappeared. Rattled, sure as hell. Out for a walk? Trying to figure out what to say about this note from Barbour, maybe. Dee reached down and found the crumpled wad in Ashley's wastebasket. When he looked up he saw Buck, with a stack of copy in his hands, sitting down at Ashley's desk.

"Amos, he just left" said Dee. "Without a word, he. . ."

"I know" said Buck. "I told him to go home."

"Go home? I thought he. . ."

"He's having trouble with his daughter. I just found out."

"Amos . . . he has a daughter? I never knew that, I. . ."

"Amy. She's been screwing around with some ex-paratrooper."

"His daughter . . . okay, a paratrooper . . . so. . ."

"Her job at the telephone company, they don't pay her much."

"Her job? That's all, Buck? That's why he been acting strange?"

"She's come up with a lot of money he can't account for, that's why."

"Damn . . . so that's what it's been all along, it's. . ."

Ashley's daughter, giving him hell, coming up with funny money, so that's why he wouldn't listen. Dee looked down at Buck, watching him start to mark copy, hearing him say "Keep it to yourself, what I just told you."

Nodding when Buck added "No more riding around with cops for a while, I want you to help on the rewrite desk while Amos takes a rest."

Seeing him look up with a frown on his face, saying "Little Bob, we'll get that bastard yet."

"The mayor . . . Buck . . . about last night. . ."

"My fault. I should not have listened to Herman."

"Herman? He was the one who tipped you off about Tyrell?"

"A big bet, a bet Tyrell was going to squeal on Little Bob."

"Herman . . . right . . . he keeps up on all the bets. I'll be damned."

Dee went back to his desk and lowered his head. Buck. Ashley. Barbour. Ashley's right, it's one damned thing after another.

"You look worn out" he heard someone say and looked up. Lulu, stopping in front of his desk, on her way to the lady's room.

"Maybe I am" said Dee. "I've been guarding the fort too long."

"You worry too much. You should be laid back, like me."

"Laid back . . . laid back, did you say?"

"That's the best way to be laid, you heard me."

Dee watched as she pranced away, looking back and grinning.

Lulu and her double meanings. The best way to be laid. Right. It's one damned thing after another.

PROPHETS

A COED WITH LONG BLACK HAIR STANDING BEHIND HIM IN line at the book store reached over his shoulder rubbing his cheek with a handkerchief smelling of perfume whispering it's too hot in here I have a motorcycle let's go for a ride in the country pointing to the sidecar telling Dee hop in driving through a forest leaping out with the engine still running saying put that mattress from the sidecar under this tree ripping off his clothes taking off her dress tight breasts bushy black hair between her legs lying down on the mattress murmuring yes, yes, yes, you have what I need, it's big and red, please, please, please, don't just stand there, give it to me, I'm your hot sweet mama, my engine's running, hear the sound of my engine, the sound of the engine, the sound of the door bell ringing, a ringing sound, ringing. . .

"All right, damn it, I'll be there" Dee yelled, crawling out of bed.

"Omar, get up, it's nine o'clock" said Debbie, looking through the screen door. "Why aren't you dressed? Why are you holding that bathrobe in front of you, what are you hiding?"

"You want to see what I'm hiding? You want to touch it?"

"No, get dressed, let's go for a ride in the country."

"I've just been for a ride in the country. You ruined it."

"Hurry up, I want to show you what free love really is."

"Free love? I'm all alone, why not show me here?"

"In the country, Omar. I'll wait downstairs."

Dee shaved, then showered, taking his time getting dressed. Sunday, the one day he can sleep past noon, so what's the hurry? Debbie, she'll wait, hell, maybe she means it. Free love in the country, under the trees, for real, not another dream. Who knows?

She was silent as she drove north from Austin. Four miles on the highway, another mile on a gravel road, her roadster bouncing up and down, Dee holding on as best he could, wondering where in hell she was going.

"It's not what you told me" said Debbie, turning into a clearing.

"Not what I told you? Free love, you mean?"

"It's not what the Commies say, Omar. Not at all."

"Fine . . . fine . . . so why are we stopping?"

"It's when you give your heart to Jesus. That's what free love is."

Dee groaned when he saw why she had stopped. Straight ahead in the clearing a country church, with twenty or thirty cars parked around it, with the sound of some old Christian hymn coming from inside. Five miles back to Austin. Trapped.

"We have to hurry, Omar. He'll be starting any minute."

"Damn it, Debbie, why have you dragged me out here?"

"Reverend John, he's changed my life around."

"Really? Who the hell is Reverend John?"

"We'll find a seat, you'll see. Behave yourself, Omar."

Behave yourself? Hell yes, it's a long walk home if you don't. So sit here and be quiet, watch the choir lead the congregation in another hymn, hear Debbie sing along, waiting for her mentor to show up, this preacher she calls Reverend John.

Dee leaned to his right and twisted his head, so he could see the preacher on the other side of the pulpit. Sitting next to the choir in a rocking chair, reading a Bible, an old man with long white hair down to his shoulders.

When the singing ended a woman in the choir helped the preacher to his feet and he hobbled to the pulpit, using a cane, looking down at his Bible. Speaking in a soft voice, saying "The Book of Proverbs, let us pray."

Dee leaned back and closed his eyes. Proverbs. Fine, a half hour sermon, the usual Amens along the way, then the donation baskets up and down the aisle, while the preacher called for folks to give their souls to Jesus. East Texas all over again.

"The path of the just is a shining light" said the preacher. "Proverbs Four Eighteen." No Amens. Odd. When the preacher quoted another line, something about transgressors, no Amens then, either. Only an outburst of applause.

Dee opened his eyes and looked around. Young people, college age, applauding as the preacher rambled on and on, about truth and justice, about taking sides, his voice getting louder. No East Texas sermon here. More like a pep rally instead.

"Ninety six years ago" said the preacher, standing beside the pulpit, waving his cane in the air. "That's how long it has been since my namesake took the first great step in setting free our colored brothers."

More applause. "That's John Brown he's talking about" said the young man sitting next to Dee, "But it's not Harper's Ferry this time, this time we'll be marching on the State Capitol, you'll see."

"A few months ago the U.S. Supreme Court ruled separate is not equal" said the preacher. "But the State of Texas will not comply. We must follow John Brown's footsteps, we must protest, do you see the signs in the back of the church?"

Dee turned and saw a woman coming in the back door, stacking signs against the wall. Signs mounted on wooden poles for marching. With the words Separate is Not Equal. Texas Must Comply. Liberate East Austin. God Is With Us.

He was still looking at the signs when he heard a voice over his shoulder. Reverend John, coming down the aisle, stopping and saying "Sister Debbie, bless your soul, you have brought a new young man to our congregation."

"I have" said Debbie. "But I don't think he's ready yet."

"You're not with the Lord?" asked the preacher, looking at Dee.

"With the Lord . . . well, not exactly" said Dee. "I'm with the paper."

"He's a writer" said Debbie. "With the Austin paper."

"Your paper, you do not report on colored people" said the preacher.

"Some of us try" said Dee. "But look, it's the publisher, he. . ."

"I shall pray for you" said the preacher, looking down at Dee, his white hair hanging over his eyes. "You must pray for him as well, Sister Debbie, this paper he works for is in league with the Devil."

Dee grunted as the preacher moved on, with Debbie right behind him. Let them march, Charlie Black will fire the poor bastard who tries to write about it. In league with the Devil? Damned right, it's owned by a man who'd play golf with the Devil.

When they got outside the church Debbie opened the rumble seat of her car and laid one of the signs in it. Justice For All. Dee watched as the others did the same, putting signs in their cars and heading for Austin, ready to march in front of the Capitol.

Ready to march, all right, but not ready to get their hands dirty. Not ready to go into East Austin and see what it's like there. Not ready to go in the alleys and clean up the trash. Not ready to take on the cops who broke into Bubba's.

"Why are you so quiet" asked Debbie as they drove away.

"These people you're marching with, a bunch of goddamn cowards."

"You curse too much, Omar. Jesus wouldn't like that."

"Jesus and Reverend John, right, they've changed your life around."

"They have. No more horsing around with boys."

"You ever read the book of Proverbs, Debbie?"

She shook her head. Maybe he should read it to her. The part he remembered from junior high school, the best part, the part about getting laid. Hell, half the Proverbs are all about screwing around with strange women. Harlots, smelling of perfume.

Forget it. Leave her alone. Let Reverend John show her how to march. No more horsing around with boys? Forget that night they drove away from the Tavern. She can be a cheerleader for Jesus now.

"You want me to drop you at home?" asked Debbie.

"At home, good. I have to write a paper for Professor Eastman."

"Why are you laughing, Omar?"

"That motorcycle that just went by, did you see it?"

"It had a side car, with a woman driving it, so what?"

"There's no motorcycles in the Book of Proverbs, Debbie."

"Of course not, what in the world are you getting at?"

"Nothing. Just a dream I had before you woke me up this morning."

Dee was still laughing as went up the steps to the apartment on Lorraine. Harlots riding around on motorcycles with sidecars, how in hell could he work that into a paper on Texas history? Only if Eastman has a sense of humor.

"This essay you have written is shallow" said the professor. "That is why I have asked you to see me in my office." Eastman, up close, older than he looks in class, almost as old as Reverend John, but with his hair trimmed short, wearing steel-rimmed glasses. Looking at Dee without a smile.

"Juneteenth . . . sir, I thought that would. . ."

"The topic you have chosen is fine, Mister Dee."

"But it's shallow? Professor, I thought. . ."

"It is not a history paper. It is more like journalism."

"Journalism . . . I suppose I. . ."

"The way you write for the newspaper, that will not do."

"You've seen my byline? Then you know I. . ."

"Yes, enough to know why you are you looking at that watch."

Eastman pointed to a watch on his desk. A watch next to a picture of his wife. The same watch Dee had seen the night of the car crash that killed her. Hanging from her wrist in the wreckage, a watch with blue and red colors on its face. The watch that disappeared minutes later, when the police took over the crash site.

The police. The two hardcore Marines, Barbour and Abrams. Bloodthirsty, gunning down that kid, the two crooked cops who stole that watch and threatened to do him in for nosing around.

"That watch belonged to my wife" said Eastman.

"I've seen it before . . . I saw it when she was. . ."

"Yes, I know you were there, I read what you wrote in the paper."

"But this watch, how did it get here?"

"A policeman brought it to me. You seem surprised."

"A policeman? A policeman, how could. . ."

"Sergeant Barbour. With tears in his eyes. Perhaps you know him."

Dee nodded, still looking at the watch. Barbour. With tears in his eyes? The same Barbour who shot that kid, and then sent that letter, saying thanks for getting him off the hook with the chief. Damn it, damn it. . .

"Now, about your essay on Juneteenth, Mister Dee. Are you listening?"

"My essay . . . right . . . right, what I turned in, I. . ."

"As I said a moment ago, it is far too much like journalism."

"Journalism . . . yessir . . . what I wrote is. . ."

"You must do some research, beyond reporting what you saw."

"Research . . . right. . ."

"A history paper must answer certain questions. The kind of questions newspapers have no time to deal with. For instance, Juneteenth, when did it begin, when did it start in East Austin?"

Eastman stood up abruptly, as if what he had said reminded him of something else. Walking around his desk, handing the essay back to Dee. Looking down at the picture of his wife, shaking his head.

"East Austin, Mister Dee. What do you know about East Austin?"

"Juneteenth, the police reports for the paper, the. . ."

"No, not that. What do you know about the voting there?"

"The voting there . . . yessir . . . I've been tracking on some hunches."

"Hunches? Not my wife. She was certain Lyndon Johnson knew."

"Senator Johnson? Your wife, she talked to him?"

"She was coming from his ranch when she was killed."

"Johnson, she saw him? Professor, what did she find out?"

"I have no idea, young man. I wish I knew."

Eastman turned away from the picture of his wife and walked to an open window, telling Dee to look out with him, pointing to a line of students in the distance. Twenty or thirty, marching back and forth in front of the University Tower, carrying signs.

"They've been at that since this morning" said Eastman.

"Too far away to read the signs" said Dee. "What are they protesting?"

"Atomic war, perhaps. It doesn't matter. See that television camera?"

"Yessir, it looks like the one I saw in the Capitol a few weeks ago."

"The question you asked, what my wife found out, there's your answer."

"The answer? Professor, I don't. . ."

"She called me after she left Johnson's ranch. Before she was killed."

"Your wife, she. . ."

"East Austin, Johnson said the voting there is all about television."

"Television? What does that mean, all about television?"

"I wish I knew, young man, I wish I knew."

Eastman walked away from the window and sat down at his desk. Holding the picture of his wife, turning around in his chair, with his back to Dee. Silent, his head lowered, looking at the picture. Deep in thought.

Dee waited for a moment, noticing again the watch on Eastman's desk, the watch Barbour had returned. He walked from the office then, closing the door as quietly as he could. Rattled. Shaking his head.

Barbour. Crooked cops. East Austin, crooked voting. Eastman's wife, saying the voting there is all about television. How in hell can that add up?

Rattled.

When the bus stopped on Congress Avenue Dee got off three blocks early, by accident, paying no attention, still rattled, with his mind on what he had heard in Eastman's office. He looked around, cursed himself, and started walking.

A crowd on the sidewalk blocked his path. Fifty people at least, clustered around the window of a department store. Dee looked up at the sign. On Sale, Latest Television Models. Zenith. Admiral. Westinghouse. Prices Lowered.

"Lowered, hell, they're still too much" said a man in front of Dee.

"Sure, but look what they're showing" said someone else.

"The World Series" said another. "Get up close and see."

"What's going on?" asked a woman walking by.

"Indians and Giants, Game One" a man answered.

"In New York, at the Polo Grounds" someone added.

"Polo. That's for rich folks" said the woman, moving on.

Dee edged his way toward the window. A half dozen TV sets showing the game. With a salesman standing behind them, holding a sign saying NBC. Fine, watch for a few minutes before going to work. Something to get his mind off Eastman.

"What's the score?" he asked.

"Tied, two to two, middle of the eighth" a man answered.

"Commercials, then they'll show that catch again" someone added.

"Damndest catch you ever seen" said another.

"Willie Mays" said someone. "For a colored player, he's really fast."

"Fast, all right" someone muttered. "He must have white blood in him."

"White blood, hell, he's got fire up his ass" said someone else.

Dee watched as the broadcast showed the play again. Mays, running backwards in deep center field, making the catch over his shoulder, spinning around, losing his cap, throwing the ball towards the infield.

"Four hundred fifty feet at least" said the announcer. As he spoke the camera panned toward the stadium seats, showing the fans on the front row cheering as the Giants ran onto the field for the bottom of the eighth.

"That's Durocher waving to his wife" said the announcer.

"Leo the Lip" said a man next to Dee. "I can't stand that bastard."

"Yeah, but look at that babe he's married to" said someone else.

"Laraine Day, that Hollywood actress" someone added.

"Durocher" someone grumbled. "He's got the world by the balls."

"You mean by the tits" someone laughed.

"Yeah, like LBJ and Lady Bird" a man behind him muttered.

Dee grunted. Idiotic talk. Someone should open a popcorn stand right here, on the sidewalk in front of this store, give these folks something to munch on while they watch TV and make stupid jokes like that.

"Hell yes, she owns the station here" said the man next to him.

"Johnson's wife? She owns the Austin station?" Dee asked.

"The only one in town" he answered. "They're getting rich."

"With all these damned commercials they keep showing" someone added.

"He'll own half of Austin by the time he's out of office" someone muttered.

"Out of office, hell" said a man behind him. "He'll be elected from now on."

"Politics. It's all crooked as shit, how they get elected" said a man in front of the window. "Including Lyndon Johnson."

Dee looked around and nodded.

Maybe all this talk is not so dumb.

Crooked politics. . .

The voting in East Austin. . .

Lady Bird owning the television station. . .

Johnson getting rich on TV commercials. . .

Eastman's wife, grilling LBJ an hour before she's killed. . .

LBJ telling her the politics in East Austin is all about television. . .

Maybe, just maybe, it's starting to add up. Bits and pieces here and there, some pieces still missing, but maybe it's starting to fit together.

He waited until the game was over. The Giants winning in the tenth on a homer, the announcer saying it was actually Mays who won it for them when he made that catch. A basket catch, he called it.

A basket catch. Damned right. Maybe he's made one himself, standing here in front of this window.

Buck, wearing his Navy cap, sat at Ashley's desk, sorting out pictures and stories, marking copy, grunting and shrugging his shoulders, looking like the skipper of a ship about to run aground.

"Amos gets back tomorrow" he muttered, looking up at Dee.

"I've got a question, Buck. About TV stations."

"Tomorrow. Not a goddamn minute too soon."

"Austin, LBJ, why does he have the only one in Austin?"

"One too many. Trash, all that Lucille Ball shit on television."

"Fine, but why only one? Does it cost too much to own one?"

"You want to buy a TV station? That bonus I gave you, use that."

"It's a simple question, damn it, why is there only one?"

Buck stood up, stretching his arms. Rubbing his eyes and his forehead. Looking down at the copy still unmarked. Muttering something about Amos and his daughter, then looking up at Dee, still waiting for an answer.

"The FCC has to issue a license to broadcast. Why do you ask?"

"FCC. Federal Communication Commission. Who's in charge?"

"Congress, really. Lomax, he's head of the committee, he. . ."

"Congressman Lomax. Right, I know, he runs East Austin."

"There's a fee, I think. Lomax, he . . . damn it, what are you on to?"

"Lyndon Johnson. Buck, there's something crooked going on."

"Something crooked. Another one of your idiot hunches."

"It's not a hunch, I've been tracking on a. . ."

"You don't need a bullet proof vest, you need a straitjacket."

"Buck, listen, Eastman's wife, before she died she. . ."

"The kind they use in the loony ward. Go away, beat it."

Buck held his hands over his ears and sat down. Dee waited, trying to think of something more to say. To hell with it, he'll look it up in the files. The FCC, the voting records, all the rest, then pile it up in front of Buck and make him listen.

He turned away abruptly, bumping into someone behind him. Rudy, the photographer at the tea dance, the one who took the shot that sent Meredith off to Hollywood. Coming from the darkroom with pictures for Buck.

The pictures spilled on the floor. Rudy bent over to pick them up, Dee said "sorry", and saw one that made him groan. A shot of Debbie Decker, legs spread apart, lying on the ground with a broken protest sign.

"What's this, cheesecake?" asked Buck when Rudy handed him the picture.

"No way" said Rudy. "It's not art, but it's sure as hell news."

"With her dress up to her waist? We can't print this, forget it."

"See the Capitol behind her? They knocked her down when she was marching."

"Marching, my ass" said Buck. "Let's see the rest of what you have."

Dee watched as Rudy laid out the pictures. In sequence. Reverend John and the others getting off a church bus. Lining up and starting to march. Some men from across the street charging at them. Broken signs, people shouting. Two policemen in the midst, herding the marchers back on the bus. Six pictures of a melee.

"The sign this woman was holding, what does it say?" asked Buck.

"Let me look" said Rudy. "Jesus loves us, maybe. It's broken."

"This man with the long white hair, what's on that sign?"

"Something about elections in East Austin. They broke that one, too."

"Elections in East Austin. Too bad. Good shots, but I can't use them."

"Why not, Buck? Because we don't cover East Austin?"

"Damn it, you're not listening. Keep them. Take them away."

Dee watched, almost certain what would happen next. Rudy starting to argue, Buck putting his hands over his ears again, Rudy waiting, then giving up, taking the pictures off the desk, walking away with his head down.

"Best shit I've shot in a month" he said. "What's wrong with Buck?"

"It's not him, it's Charlie Black" said Dee.

"Black? What does he want? Some more pictures of his golf clubs?"

"He's taken over the elections. Everything has to go through him."

"That bastard. You ask me, he's the one the cops should nail."

"Cops. Wait. Rudy, how old are these pictures? When did you. . ."

"After lunch, one thirty maybe, that's when these two cops waded in."

"Four hours ago. I'll be damned."

Dee went back to his desk and picked up the phone. Bothered. Working the rewrite desk, keeping up with The Blotter by calling the precinct station, and not a word about two policemen breaking up a crowd in front of the Capitol?

"No report on that" said the desk sergeant on the phone.

"Four hours ago, you would know by now. . ."

"We'd have known right away, that's procedure."

"Okay . . . wait . . . do you know who was in that area? Two police. . ."

"None of our guys. They've been on patrol all day."

"Two police, from some other precinct, maybe?"

"No way, the chief would have their ass. Somebody's been pulling your leg."

Pulling his leg, hell, something's going on. Forget the FCC. A mess in front of the Capitol, no big deal, but if it's being covered up by a couple of cops . . . damn it, that shot Rudy took, the two policemen, they're in those pictures. . .

Dee leaped up and headed for the darkroom. The red warning light above the door meant wait, so he waited. And waited. And then started knocking on the door. Dinner time, damn it, Rudy's up to his usual tricks, he's in there eating.

Right on. After two more knocks the light went off, the door opened and Rudy came out, with a bag of chips in one hand and a soft drink in the other, chewing away, with his mouth full, having a hard time trying to speak.

"For Chrissake, Dee, give me a break, I might have had a babe in here."

"Might have, sure. I need to see those pictures, Rudy."

"Which ones, the porno prints I've been working on?"

"Porno, hell. The pictures at the Capitol, where are they?"

"That shit Buck turned down, upstairs, on the table."

"In the morgue? That mess? Damn it, Rudy, show me."

"Okay, you don't want to see my nudes, okay."

Dee followed as Rudy went up the stairs. To the morgue, munching on potato chips, like some teenager at a picnic, even if he's thirty or so. The best cameraman in town, but gone for sure, if Buck finds out he's printing porno in the darkroom.

The morgue. Rudy turned on the lights and Dee looked around. Two rows of file cabinets, a copy machine, a typewriter, a long table in the middle, stacks of newspapers, piles of clippings ready to be filed. A mess from end to end.

"The babe who works in here, she holding down two jobs" said Rudy.

"Good for her. What about those pictures?"

"All night at the phone company, then she's in here at dawn."

"The pictures of the cops, where are they?"

"I asked her once if she wanted to earn some extra dollars. When I mentioned posing in the nude she poured coffee on me."

Rudy mumbled the woman's name, Wanda something or other, and walked to the end of the table. Looking around, finding an envelope marked To Be Filed, pulling out the pictures and handing them to Dee. Mumbling Wanda, she's too much.

"These two pictures of the cops. Rudy, all you can see is their backs."

"Their backs, sure, running across the street, then raising hell."

"Nothing with their faces, their name tags, that's all you took?"

"That shot of the babe on the ground, that's not bad, look at that."

"No . . . no . . . the two policemen . . . I need to know who they were."

"Cheesecake, that's what Buck said. I wonder if she'd like to model."

"Forget it, she's into Jesus. Hell, maybe she can put a word in for you.."

Dee sat down at the end of the table. Beat. Two cops, going after some signs about the voting in East Austin, that could have been a big-time break. But no ID on the cops, dead end, one more hunch out the window. To hell with these pictures.

"Lost cause, Rudy. I might as well stick to the rewrite desk."

"Okay, but you don't need to throw my pictures all over the table."

"Maybe I'll keep the one of the lady on the ground. Where did it go?"

"Over there, on top of that empty folder. The one marked FCC."

Dee got up and went to the middle of the table. The FCC folder, empty all right, with a typewritten note inside. Saying the contents of this file have been transferred to the office of the publisher, Charles Black. With the initial W at the bottom.

Black. The FCC file, why would he take that? Nothing but clippings for sure. How they granted Lyndon Johnson's TV franchise, maybe, but so what? Black's not going after LBJ, the paper's on his side. Or maybe, just maybe. . .

"You look puzzled, Dee. Snake bit, that's what Hattie calls it."

"Snake bit? Hattie? What are you talking about?"

"That babe at Hattie's, Ginger, I wanted to take some shots of her."

"Ginger, right. Nude pictures, damn it, Rudy, you. . ."

"Hattie said I could screw her, but no pictures of her naked."

"Hell no, naked pictures, Rudy, that's against the law."

"That's what Hattie said, she said I looked snake bit when she told me."

Enough. Dee waked away, leaving Rudy mumbling about nude photos. Back at his desk he wrote a note to call Debbie and see how she is, then put her picture in a drawer, on top of the Split Rail Poster and some other junk. Shaking his head.

Snake bit. Black with the FCC files, useless pictures of two cops, Buck dumping crap on his desk for rewrite, a bad day only half way over.

No basket catch at all. Snake bit.

Alone and unsettled, with the final edition on the streets and the city room deserted, he looked down at the pile of books his desk and nodded. The Juneteenth paper for Eastman, get back to that, anything to get his mind off what kept nagging him. Some kind of missing link, something to tie it all together. What LBJ told Eastman's wife. East Austin, it's all about television, the voting in East Austin.

"What are you doing here so late?" asked Buck, coming from his office.

"Looking at some books for a history class. Trying to get organized."

"You? Organized? You're as screwed up as Ashley."

"You said he's coming back tomorrow . . . what about his daughter"

"Amy? He's still worried about that money she came by, he's. . ."

"Her job at the telephone company, hell, maybe she saved it."

"No, Amos thinks it has something to do with this guy she's been seeing."

"An ex-paratrooper, you said. You know, Buck, I have a hunch it could be. . ."

"Sure, as dumb as the hunch you had about that East Austin poster."

"That poster from the Split Rail? Amos said forget it, but listen, Buck. . ."

"You and your hunches. Keep it up, some day you'll get us all fired."

Buck headed for the elevator, muttering something about Charlie Black and East Austin and the next election. Dee rummaged through his desk drawer, looking for the Split Rail poster. With a one dollar bill clipped to it, overlooked. All that's left from that bonus from Black. A memento. Something to laugh about. Whatever.

Memento, hell, go back to square one. Forget this history paper for now, track on that poster. Find Ashley's buddy Liebwitz, find out what he knew about the voting in East Austin. The poster, that's it, go downstairs and see if there's anyone still there, some printer who might know where it was made.

They were there, all right. Two printers walking past him, groaning, looking back, over their shoulders, one of them saying Dee stay out of that game, Jake's been on a roll all night, he's stripped me of everything but my frigging underwear.

And three others, standing around a blanket spread across a make-up table. D-Day paratroopers, all three. Jake and Dummy, printers now, heroes at Normandy. And Arnie, a hero of sorts, as well. From the fifty yard line in Memorial Stadium.

"Last hand, you want in?" asked Jake when Dee approached them.

"No, it's this poster" said Dee. "I need to know where it was made."

"That thing with a dollar on it? Get in, I'll look at it later."

"Hell, why not? I've been losing all day, maybe my luck will change."

Five card stud. With Jake dealing. And talking to Arnie. But not to Dummy, deaf since Normandy. With Dee not listening at all, looking at the first two cards Jake dealt him. An ace in the hole, another one up.

"So you're going to settle down" said Jake to Arnie. "Going to tie the knot."

"Damned right" said Arnie. "We've got the marriage license already."

"I'll open for a dollar" said Dee. "Deal the cards."

"So when's the wedding?" asked Jake.

"Not sure" said Arnie. "She's afraid to ask her dad."

Dummy tossed a dollar in the pot and Jake yelled in his ear, as loud as he could, Arnie's getting married. Dummy grinned and took a notebook from his pocket, writing something and handing it to Jake. While Dee waited, looking at his cards.

"Arnie, it's for you" said Jake, patting Dummy on the back.

"For me? What's he saying, don't bet against that ace?"

"No, he says you get married, he's got a wedding present for you."

"I don't need a present" said Arnie. "I need better cards."

"He says he'll give you a puppy, not even housebroken yet."

"Dogs" Arnie laughed. "I'll call you Dee, with this. It's worth a dollar."

"With that?" asked Dee. "What is it?"

"A raffle ticket. The mayor, he's raffling off a brand new Cadillac."

"Screw the mayor" said Dee, reaching for his wallet. "I'll raise another dollar."

Arnie looked at his cards and folded. So did Jake and Dummy. Dee raked in the pot. Ahead by two dollars and a raffle ticket so far. So far, hell, they were done, he could see, as soon as Dummy walked away and Arnie said he was finished.

"You're broke?" asked Dee. "What about all that money I heard you won?"

"Right on the fifty yard line" said Arnie. "Nobody thought we could pull that off."

"I heard they bet against it big time" said Jake. "So how much did you win?"

"Six hundred bucks, Amy's got it stashed away, all of it."

"Amy?" Dee blurted out. "Ashley's daughter? That's who was with you?"

"Damned right" said Arnie. "We're ready to get married, too. Except. . ."

"So she's afraid to ask him" said Jake. "Why don't you ask him yourself?"

"Not me" Arnie replied. "Amy says he's in a damned bad mood, wanting to know where she got that money. He'd grill me, too. No way, I can't ask him."

Dee grunted. Ashley, coming back tomorrow. In a damned bad mood, all right. A pain in the ass to work for. And likely to stay that way until this crap about his darling Amy gets settled, one way or the other. So what the hell, give it a shot.

"You won't need to ask him" said Dee. "I'll do it for you."

"Great . . . great . . . but what if he asks you about. . ."

"About that bet? Don't worry, I'll figure out something."

Arnie stepped around the table and shook Dee's hand. While Jake patted Dee on the back, smiling, telling Arnie to go home and keep his fingers crossed. Not smiling when he looked at the poster Dee had handed him.

"What's this? The coming election in East Austin won't be democratic?"

"I need to know where that was printed, Jake. That's all."

"Why? You won't be able to write about it. Black won't let you."

"The election, all his, right. You've heard about that, have you?"

"Word gets around. What's that bastard up to?"

"See where that was printed. Maybe we'll find out."

Dee turned to walk away, but Jake said wait, still looking at the poster, turning it over, holding it against the light, shaking his head, then nodding, with a look on his face that could only mean he was on to something.

"One of three or four places. I'll check around, Phil."

"The man who had it made, that's who I'm after."

"You had a dollar bill clipped to it, what was that for?"

"The last dollar from a bonus I got. From Black, believe it or not."

"A bonus from that bastard, I'll be damned."

"A bonus, right, so what are you laughing about?"

"With that dollar from Black you won a lottery ticket, so now win the car, hell yes, serve that sonofabitch right."

Dee headed for the stairwell, leaving Jake behind him, still laughing. Screw the lottery ticket, forget it, what are the odds? Odds, hell. It's Arnie now, what are the odds he can come up with something to tell Ashley about his darling daughter?

SNIFFING DOGS

Ashley would not be easy to deal with. That was clear enough from the way he was leaning forward in his swivel chair, rubbing his jaw, thumbing through the last few days of the paper, almost growling when he looked up at Dee.

"I see you've been on rewrite while I was out."

"Plus the Blotter, Amos."

"So what do you want? A medal for good behavior?"

The Blotter, right. Tell him about the police in front of the Capitol, then get around to what he's really here for. Arnie and his daughter. But warm him up first. With a word or two about the poster and his buddy Liebwitz. If he'll only listen. . .

"Forget that poster, damn it. I've told you a dozen times, that's off limits."

"Okay, but if I can find out where Abe is, we'll be able to. . ."

"Piss on Abe" muttered Ashley, rubbing his jaw again. "Who's this with you?"

"With me? There's nobody with me Amos, I. . ."

There was indeed someone with him. Dee felt the pat on his shoulder and turned around. Arnie, dressed in a suit and tie, standing right behind him, at parade rest, looking like he was ready to go to war again.

"Arnie, what are you doing here?" asked Dee, almost whispering.

"I can't let you speak for me" said Arnie. "That would be a coward's way out."

"Who the hell are you?" asked Ashley, rubbing his jaw and looking up at Arnie.

"He's Arnold Evans" said Dee. "I interviewed him back in June, I. . ."

"In June? Four months ago? What are you talking about?" said Ashley.

"He's the nephew of the UT athletic director" said Dee. "He's. . ."

"That's me, all right" said Arnie, looking down at Ashley. "And I'm here to tell you flat out, I'm going to marry your daughter, with or without your okay."

"You're that paratrooper she's been fooling around with" said Ashley, standing up and shouting. "Like hell you are. Where'd she get that money?"

"Amos, damn it, calm down" said Dee. "Arnie gave it to her."

"You stay out of this" muttered Ashley, rubbing his jaw again, looking around the city room. Quiet, with the whole crowd staring at him. Then noisy again, back to work, typewriters clattering when they saw the managing editor coming from his office.

"What's all this yelling about?" asked Buck, looking straight at Dee.

"It's nothing" Dee answered. "We were just. . ."

"So you're the famous Arnold Evans" said Buck, looking now at Arnie.

"Famous? No, I. . ." Arnie stuttered.

"You three, come with me" ordered Buck. "In my office."

They followed. Ashley first, Arnie right behind him, Dee marching slowly in the rear. Uneasy. Caught off guard. No way to get Ashley on board with Arnie, no way to play Cupid now. Not with Buck in charge.

"Your jaw's still hurting you?" asked Buck, looking at Ashley.

"I'll get over it" said Ashley. "If I. . ."

"An abscessed tooth, you should have gone to a better dentist."

Ashley grunted, saying nothing. While Buck sat down and spun his chair around, looking at the pictures on the wall behind his desk. Tapping one with his finger, the picture of a Navy ship. Then turning around and smiling.

"Amos, it's time to let her go" said Buck.

"I know, I know" said Ashley, looking down at the floor and speaking softly.

"Arnold made a bet, that's how Amy got that money, so forget it."

"All right . . . whatever you say . . . I. . ."

"He wants to marry her, right?"

"So he claims, Buck."

"If we were at sea, I could marry them myself, you know that."

"I suppose you could, yes, but. . ."

"But we're not at sea" said Buck. "So here's what you do. Take a pill, stop that jaw from hurting, and go work it out with Arnold. Two weeks from tomorrow, that's my birthday. A wedding in Memorial stadium, right on the fifty yard line."

Arnie had said nothing, looking back and forth at Buck and Ashley as they spoke. Awed, perhaps, at Buck's commanding voice. Now he said thanks, reached forward and shook Buck's hand, and followed Ashley out of the office without another word.

Dee watched them leave, then turned and looked at Buck. Puzzled. How did Buck know about that fifty yard line bet? How did he know Arnie wanted to marry Ashley's daughter? And Ashley, what's this about an abscessed tooth?

"I don't get it, Buck. Why did Amos cave in like that?"

"Cave in? It's that tooth, it's been giving him fits."

"But Amy, he's been raising hell about that money she. . ."

"Forget it" said Buck. "That's all settled now." Forget it, hell. Dee shook his head, still wondering. Watching Buck shuffle through some papers on his desk, then reaching for a note stuck on a spindle, looking up at Dee and smiling again.

"Hattie called. She has a picture for you. Something important."

"A picture? Important? Okay, I'll get a ride out there tonight and. . ."

"I'll take you. Herman told me I should be there."

"Herman, still covering bets. . ."

"An old millionaire from Atlanta" said Buck, almost laughing. "Blind, with a seeing eye dog, back in town for a class reunion.

He's told them he's going out there tonight, Herman's covering bets on whether Hattie will let him in."

A seeing eye dog? A millionaire going out to Hattie's? Who gives a damn? Dee looked down at Buck, starting to reach for his phone, then putting it down and looking up again. Not smiling now.

"But that's not why I need to be there. Senator Johnson wants to see me."

"LBJ? At Hattie's?"

"On his way to Houston. Something about Charlie Black, I think."

"Black, fine, but I still don't get it. Amos, that tooth he had pulled, it. . ."

"Some dentist he knew before. Some quack named Liebwitz."

"Liebwitz? You're sure that's who. . ."

"Hell yes, I'm sure. Now get back to work, we'll go out there tonight."

Dee walked back to his desk and looked around. Ashley gone, off with Arnie maybe, putting together a wedding for Buck's birthday. Liebwitz still in town and pulling teeth, a seeing eye dog at Hattie's, LBJ and Charlie Black, damn. . .

Too much. Too much to swallow.

The Pink House. Three in the morning, still crowded in the downstairs room. A couple going up the stairs, another couple coming down, Buck sitting with LBJ and Hattie at a corner table, talking, while Dee stood at the bar and waited.

Hattie, in a bright pink dress as always, coming to the bar, reaching in her purse for a photograph, pushing it across the bar to Dee, sipping on a glass of iced tea while he studied it. A Polaroid picture, with a date along the bottom, the date it was taken.

"Ginger took it" said Hattie. "I just found out about it."

"I'll be damned" said Dee. "So Galloway was right."

"That's him, with the mayor. Look who's stepping on his hat."

"His aide, Jack and Steve they both said it was. . ."

"That's not his aide, kid. That's Congressman Lomax."

"Lomax, right, he runs East Austin. Hattie, what do you know about him? "

"He's crooked, I heard he's taking bribes for TV stations."

Dee pushed his drink away. Stay sober, add it up. Lomax, in charge of the FCC committee in Congress. Taking bribes, Hattie says. With the mayor in this picture, two months ago. The mayor, this picture, there's something about it. . .

"Hattie, you said Ginger took this. I need to ask her something."

"She's over there. In the corner. See her?"

Dee looked. Ginger, blonde and slim, and damned expensive. Talking with a customer. Not his type, but smart. Writes poetry, someone said. Studied philosophy at the university, someone said. Right. A hooker who takes pictures now.

"You need to ask her something" said Hattie. "What?"

"This picture, does she have other copies of it?"

"Two, she gave one to that fellow who runs the college magazine."

"The editor of the Ranger? She knows him?"

"She knows him, all right. He's one of her regulars."

The Ranger. The mayor, trying to shut it down, no wonder. Tyrell, what did he say that night he was eating the banana? They can't shut it down, the editor's his friend, there's another picture . . . there's. . .

"That dog! What's it doing in here?" shouted Hattie as Dee looked up.

"Winning a bet for someone" answered Dee, not loud enough for Hattie to hear.

A seeing eye dog, all right, just as Buck had said. A German Shepherd, leading a blind man through the room. An old man, older than old, holding on as the dog sniffed around. Sniffing at Ginger. Who, with a smile on her face, led them to the stairs.

Hattie said nothing. Shaking her head. While the crowd applauded, watching the old man try to climb the stairs, holding on to the dog as Ginger led them slowly, step by step, to a bedroom on the second floor.

Dee watched, then saw Buck motioning to him. Buck, having a drink with LBJ, both of them applauding, too. Dee brought his drink from the bar, sat down next to Buck, and kept his mouth shut. Let them do all the talking.

"I remember now, this young man was at the D-Day celebration" said the Senator.

"He was" said Buck. "I bit his ass about the story he wrote."

"All about the Army, as I recall. Nothing about the Navy."

"He's growing up. He's riding around in police cars now."

"Chasing crooks" said the Senator, speaking in his usual Texas drawl. A long pause then, while Johnson stared at Dee, then reached across the table and grabbed him by the shoulder. Holding on, the way he did business in Washington.

"Congressman Lomax" said the Senator. "You know who that is?"

"I do . . . yes . . . I've never met him, but I know who he is" said Dee.

"That sonofabitch, he's the biggest crook of all, he. . ."

Johnson broke off in mid-sentence, hearing the noise from up above. Ginger, screaming, coming down the stairs with the dog behind her, holding an envelope in her hands, running across the room to Hattie.

"That old man, he's dead" shouted Ginger.

"Dead? Nobody dies in my house" said Hattie.

"Well, he did" moaned Ginger. "He put this envelope on a table and he was trying to get undressed and he just dropped dead." As she spoke she leaned against the bar, crying, handing the envelope to Hattie.

For a moment the room was quiet. The crowd silent, some of them watching the dog, looking lost at the bottom of the stairs. Some of them watching Ginger, looking lost as well. Not the Senator. He was looking at Dee. And giving orders.

"Young man, get over there" said Johnson. "Tell Hattie to call the sheriff."

"Senator, you should go" said Buck. "Before they. . ."

"Tell Hattie, if the sheriff gives her any trouble let me know" said Johnson.

"I'll do that, Senator . . . yessir, I'll tell her" said Dee.

"I'm on my way to Houston" said Johnson, turning to Buck. "When I get back I'll tell you what that bastard Charlie Black is really after." With that he was gone, out of Hattie's, while Dee looked at the envelope Ginger had handed her.

"I can't find my reading glasses" said Hattie. "What is it?"

"It looks like a will" said Dee. "Five or six pages, it "

"A will? What should I. . ."

"Call your lawyer. Leland, he'll know what to do."

"Leonard, yes. . ."

"And listen, when the sheriff gets here, don't tell him you have this will. Let Leland take care of it." Hattie nodded. Nobody dies in her house? Somebody did, and she was shaken. Taking advice from a reporter she calls kid, hell, that proves it.

"Let's go" said Buck. "I don't want to answer questions when the sheriff gets here." Dee followed, looking back at Hattie, hiding the will in her purse. A hell of a night, not something for the Blotter, but a hell of a night, even so.

"That picture Hattie gave you, important was it?" asked Buck as they drove away.

"Two months old, the mayor with Lomax, I'm not sure, but. . ."

"The mayor. That bastard, too bad it's not a picture of him with Charlie Black."

"Black? You said Johnson was going to tell you. . ."

"Television. He was just getting around to it when that mess broke out."

"TV? Damn, Hattie said Lomax is taking bribes for. . ."

"We'll know when I see the Senator again" said Buck, not listening. "And don't tell Hattie he's coming back, she's got enough to worry about." Dee nodded. Poor Hattie, a dead man on her hands, left with his will and his dog and who knows what else?

Enough to worry about, all right.

Lulu, sitting at Ashley's desk, looked up as Dee walked in the city room. Galloway out of town, Parker off watching movies, no way to show them this picture from Hattie's, the mayor, with Lomax stomping on Galloway's hat. And now Lulu to put up with.

"Where's Amos" he asked. "What are you doing at his desk?"

"Answering the phone. You should give me a ring some time."

"Sure, if you lend me a dime to make the call. When will Amos be back?"

"I don't know, but he's been looking for you. Jake's been looking for you, too. He left you this." Another poster. Liebwitz again. Warning East Austin not to vote for Lomax, he will steal the election. Something more for Black's embargo. Fast work by Jake, but wasted.

"Jake" said Lulu. "You know what we called a jake in the Navy?"

"This poster . . . no, I don't know what you called a jake, and I don't. . ."

"Something big and red. You had to check to see if it leaked."

"Fine . . . fine, Lulu . . . but. . ."

"A bad sign if it leaked, that meant something was wrong with it."

Something wrong if it leaks? Nothing wrong with the intercom on Ashley's desk. Buck's voice, telling Lulu to watch for Dee and send him to his office, Lulu smiling, quiet now as Dee walked away, wondering. In the Navy, what the hell is a jake?

No telling. No telling why Buck would want to see him, either. Buck, pacing back and forth, with Ashley standing near him, that much Dee could tell as he approached Buck's office. Something going on behind closed doors.

"What's that in your hand?" Buck asked when he entered. Angry.

"A poster, it. . ."

"To hell with posters. Last night, what did Hattie tell you about Lomax?"

"Hattie? In that picture, she said that's Lomax with the mayor."

"The mayor. That's damned odd, too. What else did she say about Lomax?"

"She said he's taking bribes for TV stations, Buck, she said. . ."

"What would Hattie know?" Ashley muttered. "She's been wrong before, she. . ."

"Maybe she would know about this, goddamn it" said Buck. Raising his voice, handing a sheet of newsprint to Ashley. A galley proof, Dee could tell, something to be printed in the paper.

"Black . . . he's endorsing Lomax?" asked Ashley, looking at the galley proof.

"Not just endorsing, damn it" said Buck. "He wants this on the front page."

"Well, sure, it's his election" said Ashley. "But the front page? We've never. . ."

"That's right" said Buck. "We've never put it on the damned front page. And Lomax, Senator Johnson says he's a crook, so what the hell is Black up to?" Buck shook his head, while Ashley turned to Dee and took the poster from his hands.

"Jake tracked on Liebwitz" said Dee. "See what it says? East Austin, don't. . ."

"I can read" said Ashley. "East Austin, don't vote for Lomax."

"Lomax and East Austin, damn" said Dee, turning to Buck. "There's something I just remembered. Upstairs in the morgue . . . Black, he's grabbed all the voting records from East Austin. There's nothing left but an empty file."

"The voting records" said Ashley. "Buck, wouldn't the state still have them?"

"Not for East Austin" said Buck. "Only the entire district Lomax represents."

"What about the Democratic Party?" asked Dee. "They keep files, they. . ."

"Forget it" said Buck. "When Senator Johnson checks in, we'll know what Black is up to. Right now, go back to work, I need to think."

Dee followed Ashley to the door, but stopped when he heard Buck mutter "Files, damn it, we kept better files in the Navy." Lulu. The Navy. That business about jakes, what was she was talking about? Well, hell, why not ask him, he would know.

"Buck, in the Navy, what was it they called a jake?" asked Dee.

"A jake? Who wants to know?" Buck replied, frowning.

"Lulu, she said if it leaks there's something wrong with it."

"A jake is a goddamn penis, you idiot. You have one that leaks?"

"No . . . not at all . . . but. . ."

"Then get the hell out of here" said Buck, pointing to the door. "And stay away from Lulu, damn it, you're too dumb for her." Dee stared at Buck, blushing. Lulu, hell, he should have known not to ask.

"Okay, so I'm dumb" said Dee as they left, with Ashley still holding the poster.

"You are, indeed" said Ashley. "You don't even know about this."

"That poster" said Dee. "Okay, but if we can find Liebwitz, maybe he'll. . ."

"I know where he is" said Ashley. "In the hospital, almost dead."

"Liebwitz? I think I can guess, he was passing out that poster and. . ."

"In East Austin, two cops beat him up. The hospital's moving him to Dallas for intensive care." Two cops. The same as Bubba's. Damn. And Ashley, at his desk now, looking at that poster. Liebwitz, warning about the voting in East Austin.

"Dee, think. Do you remember who first put you on to this?"

"The crooked voting in East Austin? Sure. That was Trembley, he. . ."

"He died last night. While you and Buck were out at Hattie's."

"Trembley? I knew he was old, but. . ."

"The funeral's Friday. Cover it, nose around, see what you can find out."

A funeral, right. A dead man at Hattie's, plus a dog and a will she's left with. And Lulu, over there in her slot at the ring, writing headlines, smiling as if she knew what an idiot he'd made of himself in Buck's office, a funeral would just about wrap it up.

"And stay away from Lulu" said Ashley. "You may be smart enough to work your way through college, but Buck is right, you're too damned dumb for her."

The city room, empty, with the final edition on the streets. Time to finish this rewrite on the history of Juneteenth. Not journalism now but something scholarly to satisfy Professor Eastman, complete with footnotes from a dozen books.

Finish it? Maybe not, as Dee looked up and saw who was standing in front of his desk. Hattie's bodyguard. He had seen him before, a big man, forty or so, leaning against her bar, sometimes hustling a rowdy customer out the door.

"Hattie sent me" said the bodyguard. "She needs to see you."

"Me? Why?" Too big to argue with. "Well, hell, whatever you say."

Dee locked his desk and followed him to his car. Not a word as they drove along Congress and crossed the bridge. The bodyguard, looking back to see if they were being followed. Then speaking softly when they reached the Pink House.

"She's been drinking" said the bodyguard. "First time in years."

"Hattie? She never drinks, except iced tea, she. . ."

"Four years ago, she got really drunk. When her son was killed."

"She had a son? She never mentioned him, she. . ."

"He was killed in Korea. He never knew about Hattie."

"What she does for a living, you mean. He never. . ."

"He was raised in an orphanage" said the bodyguard. Adding "Catholic, I think" as he parked behind the Pink House. Dee got out of the car, seeing Hattie sitting at a table on a porch, hearing the bodyguard say "You take care of her, she trusts you."

She was not alone, Dee could tell as he walked from the car to the porch. The seeing eye dog was there, as well. Hattie, with a drink in one hand, petting the dog with her other hand, the dog unleashed, lying on the floor beside her.

"So what's his name?" asked Dee, sitting down and pointing to the dog. Not that he cared. Just something to break the ice, get her started, find out why she sent for him, what she's. . .

"Bruno. That's what Ginger told me. Here, pour yourself a drink."

"I will, yes. So Ginger, she. . ."

"Ginger, nothing but a high-priced whore. And me, I'm nothing but her madam."

"Well . . . sure, so. . ."

"But my sister . . . she was a nun . . . she was on her way to see me." Hattie, looking up at the stars as she spoke. Washing down her words with bourbon. While Dee looked down at his glass, wondering why her bodyguard had brought him to her porch.

"Your sister. She. . ."

"She's dead. She was killed in a plane crash this afternoon."

"Hattie, I'm sorry. That's why you're. . ."

"Near Chicago, I think that's what they said."

Hattie, getting drunk, holding onto the dog, Dee reaching across the table and touching her hand, what could he say? Nothing. The Pink House madam, famous in a way, her son dead without ever knowing about her, her sister a nun, and now she's dead, too, nothing to say, nothing to do except reach across the table and hold her hand.

The dog growled when he touched her. Dee pulled his hand back, watching Hattie as she looked at the dog and opened her purse, taking out a picture and the envelope Ginger had given her, the old man's will. His seeing eye dog, Bruno, guarding a new master now. No longer growling with the picture and the envelope in her hand.

"So now I have a dog" Hattie muttered. "That's what this will says."

"Leland, he's read it?"

"Last night. He came out to see Ginger."

"Ginger? About this dog? She was the one who. . ."

"No, about that damned picture she took."

"That Polaroid? The one with Lomax and. . ."

"That's why the mayor's trying to shut down that magazine."

"The Ranger? They have a copy of that picture, sure, but. . ."

"The mayor, he's protecting Lomax, that's what Leonard said."

"Hattie, I don't get it. Why would. . ."

"To hell with Ginger's picture, look at this one. That's my sister a few years ago."

Hattie, pouring another drink, wiping tears from her cheeks, looking at the picture herself before she handed it to Dee. A nun, all right. Posing with a young man. Maybe Hattie's son, before Korea. Don't ask, let it go. And don't ask about that other picture, either. The one Ginger took. The mayor with Lomax.

The mayor . . . he's protecting Lomax? Why? From what? What's that crooked bastard up to? Right, let it go. A funeral to cover in a few hours, old Trembley, hell, his widow will be weeping, too. So get drunk with Hattie, hold her hand. If this damn dog will stop growling.

At noon Dee stood beneath a tree, at the edge of a crowd surrounding Trembley's coffin. Forty or fifty policeman standing at attention as a chaplain delivered a farewell sermon. The Police Chief making a speech about the old days, then presenting a folded Texas flag to Trembley's widow, sitting in a chair, staring at her husband's coffin.

Dee stood in the line of mourners moving past her, each stopping for a moment to offer condolences. Dee was ready to tell her he had not forgotten, he was still working on what her husband had said about East Austin. But she did not look up. No sign of recognition, so he mumbled "A good man" and moved on.

All very solemn. Quiet, as the police walked back to their squad cars. The Chief, seeing Dee and nodding, handing a note to the desk sergeant from the downtown precinct, then walking away with two men in civilian suits. Barbour and Abrams maybe, hard to tell in the distance. Dee walked away, too, heading back to the paper.

He was almost out of the cemetery, wondering what he might write about Trembley's funeral, when he heard a voice behind him, someone saying wait, I have a message for you. The desk sergeant, out of breath from chasing Dee across the cemetery lawn. Pausing for a second, then reading the Chief's note out loud.

"Tomorrow night, Scholz Beer Garden, ten o'clock" said the sergeant.

"That's from your boss?" asked Dee. "Meet him? For what?"

"I don't know. All I know is you're wrong about the Chief."

"Really? The crooked voting in East Austin? Wrong about that?"

The sergeant stared at Dee for a moment, then looked down at the grass, evidently figuring out what to say. When he looked up again he said come on, I'll give you a ride back, there's something I want to show you, something I want you to look into, maybe that will change your mind.

Dee nodded. Silent as they drove past City Hall, where a Cadillac was parked on a platform out front, with a huge sign saying Buy Raffle Tickets Here, Your Dollar Will Go to The Children's Orphanage Charity Even If You Don't Win. Dee grunted.

Charity, hell, more likely it will go to the mayor and his cronies.

Two blocks further on, the sergeant stopped in front of the Democratic Party headquarters. More signs out front. Vote For

Senator Johnson. Keep LBJ In Office. Democrats Stick With Johnson. The same signs all over Austin. All over Texas, no doubt. As if Johnson needed signs. No way. This time it would be a real landslide.

"You worry about crooked voting" said the sergeant. "Have you been in there?"

"No, I. . ." Dee started to answer. Hell no, he hadn't, Buck said don't bother.

"Maybe you're not such a smart reporter after all."

"Maybe I'm not. So why are we stopping here?"

"Go in" said the sergeant. "Ask Louella to show you the voting records."

"For East Austin? Louella?"

"See what she says. But don't tell her I sent you."

The sergeant drove away, leaving Dee on the sidewalk. He looked up at the signs again and went in. A half dozen women in the office, stacking posters, talking on telephones, most of them middle aged, busy with politics. Maybe less boring than staying at home with grandkids. Or whatever. So which one is Louella?

"I'm Louella" said one of them when he asked. "You're from the paper?"

"Right" he answered. "Phillip Dee. How did you know that?"

"I saw your picture in the paper, the one with that goofy sorority girl."

"That was a while ago. You must have a good memory, Louella, you. . ."

"I do, and I can guess why you're here. It's about all these posters."

"No, not that. It's about the voting records for East Austin."

She looked puzzled for a moment, then turned around and went to a cabinet, bringing back a thick notebook, a log book of some sort, flipping through the pages, shaking her head at what she read, then looking up at Dee with a frown on her face. A frown that told him the desk sergeant had sent him here for a damned good reason.

"The police took them. Two weeks ago. They were supposed to return them. . ."

"The police? Really? Louella, do you remember who they were?"

"They didn't wear name plates. That's odd, isn't it, they're supposed to. . ."

"Odd? Maybe, maybe not, but. . ."

"I do remember their names, what they called each other."

"That would help. A lot. . ."

"I have it written down here. Holmes. The other one was Watson."

"Holmes and Watson. You're sure."

"They said the police were checking on something, they needed the records. . ."

Dee smiled. They needed the records, all right. To cover the crooked voting In East Austin. When he heard her say she would cal the Police Department and see why they have not returned the records, he started to say forget it, they're gone. Instead he said thanks, he would write about her posters some other time, and left.

Holmes and Watson. The two cops Hattie warned about, the two he had checked on months ago. No one in the Police Department with those names. So who are they? And who are they working for? Little Bob, the mayor? Or Lomax? Or maybe even Charlie Black? Whoever, it's someone who wants those damned voting records squashed.

Outside the building he looked back at the LBJ election posters. Not a single poster for Lomax or the Mayor, they're Democrats, and they're up for election, too. What did Johnson say at Hattie's? Lomax is a crook. So the Senator would see there's no posters for Lomax. But what could he have against Little Bob?

Tomorrow night. The beer garden. Maybe the Chief will know. The way the desk sergeant talked, he's ready to open up.

Until then, work on that damned history paper for Eastman. And keep quiet about what he's just found out. Hell yes, Buck said forget it, anyway.

And he always does what Buck tells him. Right? Right.

Saturday night, on an open air stage at Scholz's Beer Garden, a young lady in a flowery dress struggled to free herself as a man wearing a black suit and a black top hat and a drooping black handlebar moustache tied her to a section of railroad track, while the sound of an onrushing train came from behind a curtain.

And a woman dressed in lederhosen stood at the side of the stage holding a stein of beer and sign that said Hiss The Villain.

Right on cue, the crowd at Scholz's hissed, and booed, and shouted "Let her go, let her go" until the young lady leaped up and threw the villain down, tying him to the track, while the sound of the onrushing train grew louder.

Seated at tables, drinking beer, they cheered then as she stood in front of the stage, holding up her arms in sign of victory as the curtain closed. Cheering, for the bad man had been run over.

Dee watched as the two stood in front of the curtain and bowed, holding steins of beer, ready for another performance in an hour. Hiss The Villain. A Saturday night tradition at Scholz's, a couple of amateur actors entertaining a packed audience.

Finding the Chief of Police would not be easy. He pushed his way among the tables, bumping into a woman in lederhosen holding a tray of steins above her head, wondering why the Chief said meet him here. And why did he want to see him, anyway?

He found him at a table under an awning, far away from the stage. Alone, wearing a civilian suit and a cowboy hat. With a hatbox on the table. When he saw Dee he motioned to the woman with the tray of steins, said bring us two beers, pushed the hatbox aside, and pointed to the empty chair at his table.

A sign for Dee to sit down. He did, and right away felt something pulling at the bottom of his trouser legs. A dog. Little. A

Pekingese, maybe, he couldn't tell in the darkness. Sniffing at his trousers, with the Chief holding the dog on a leash.

"She belongs to my nephew" said the Chief. "I keep her in this hatbox for him."

"Really. You brought me here to show me your nephew's dog?"

"My nephew is the one who plays the villain. He's a total ham."

"I wouldn't know. So what is it you really want to see me about?

"Trembley. You were right. He was on to something."

"The crooked voting in East Austin? He said the police were in on that."

"No doubt about it. That's why I asked you here. I need your help on this."

Dee leaned back, surprised. He's asking for help, after all the damned threats he made? The woman with the tray set two steins on the table, the Chief handed her a dollar bill, and Dee was even more surprised to hear what kind of help he was asking for, all ears as he spelled it out.

"It's the Mayor" said the Chief. "I'm afraid he's the real villain here."

"Little Bob? What about him?"

"I've known for years he was making bribes to get things done for Austin. . ."

"That's what my editor says. He thought that fellow Tyrell was going to squeal."

"This is something worse. It looks like Little Bob is using bribes to get elected."

"Bribes? Wait . . . you're losing me . . who's he bribing?"

"Congressman Lomax, he runs East Austin. Hell, he even has a Negro mistress."

"So Little Bob bribes Lomax to swing the vote his way? That must take. . ."

"It takes a lot of money. That's what this lottery is for. Money to bribe Lomax."

"The Cadillac he's raffling off? And you want me to help expose him? How?"

"The money from the lottery, it's supposed to go to a charity. . ."

"Right, that's what the sign at City Hall says."

"Follow where it really goes. You're a reporter, you can dig around. I can't."

"Dig around? Hell, I've been digging for months, I've been. . ."

"Look, I've been loyal to the Mayor, but no longer, damn it. He's crooked."

Dee sipped his beer, watching the Chief lean over and pour some water in a saucer for the dog. A Pekingese he keeps in a hat box for his nephew, hell, maybe he's not such a mean sonofabitch after all. All right, do what he asks, follow the lottery, see where that leads. But check on some loose ends first. A lot of loose ends.

"Okay, I'll do it, Chief. But I've got a question about Trembley, what he said."

"About cops being in on the crooked voting in East Austin? He was right."

"Dirty cops. Fine, so who's running them? Little Bob?"

"Maybe, maybe Lomax. They may be working together."

"Maybe, hell. Hattie gave me a picture that proves it, Chief."

"Hattie, I know, she called me, she. . ."

"That's her, and this picture shows them together at her place. Little Bob's trying to keep the college magazine from printing it, he's protecting Lomax, her lawyer says.."

The Chief took a notepad from his pocket and wrote something down, flipping the page and writing some more. The he put the notepad away and said that's interesting, right now he's more concerned with who these dirty cops might be.

"We don't know who they are" said the Chief. "They're using fake names."

"Holmes and Watson, I'll bet. That's something else Hattie put me on to."

"Hattie, that's what she told me, too. Holmes and Watson."

"This lottery scam, my guess is that may lead us to them."

"I have a couple looking for them now. Working undercover in East Austin."

"Abrams and Barbour, right. I saw them at the funeral."

"You figured that out? You're pretty smart, Dee. So is Barbour."

"I know . . . I was wrong about him . . . Barbour's okay, I know now."

"He's smart enough to get in tight with Lomax. So get this, he says Lomax is bragging about being in bed with your publisher."

Dee spilled his beer, speechless, hearing the Chief say you look shocked. Hearing him add hell, your paper endorsed him, didn't it, right on the front page, don't tell me your editors weren't in on that, so why are you so surprised?

"Buck and Ashley, look, Chief, they were forced to. . ."

"Something else. You have a guy on your paper named Jake?"

"He's a printer . . . what about him?"

"He called me. He wants to borrow six rifles next Tuesday."

"Rifles? What the hell for?"

"For a wedding, paratroopers with crossed rifles, he said."

"The wedding, sure. Memorial Stadium, Buck and Ashley set it up."

"I'll bring them. A wedding plus this Hiss The Villain crap, nothing better."

Dee nodded, got up, shook hands with the Chief, said he had work to do and headed back to the office. Hiss The Villain? Damn, there must be at least three villains now. Black, Lomax, Little Bob, and maybe more.

But not Buck and Ashley. They're not villains. Oh no, Lomax in bed with Black, they'll hug him when he tells them what the Chief has just said about Black.

Like hell they will. So screw it. Don't tell them.

Dee handed his Juneteenth paper to Eastman at the end of class, looked at his watch, and walked as fast as he could across campus, pushing his way through another student protest about something or other, on his way to the football stadium, rushing to a wedding the whole city was buzzing about.

He waited for traffic to pass in front of the stadium, then started across and saw Herman, on the sidewalk, looking at the morning paper. At the entertainment section, where Parker had put their pictures, Arnie and Ashley's daughter Amy, teasing the paper's readers with a mystery story: why are they getting married on the 50 yard line?

"So what are the odds?" asked Dee. "With no bright lights to worry about?"

"Ten to one they'll have their clothes on this time" said Herman.

"If they don't, that would make a hell of a picture in the paper, right?"

"You want odds, wait until you hear what Hopalong Tyrell is up to."

"Tyrell? Whatever it is, I don't want to know" said Dee.

Herman laughed as he followed him into the stadium, where a hundred or more had gathered around a minister holding a Bible, ready to start the ceremony. Ten to one, indeed, with Arnie dressed in a suit and tie and Ashley's daughter in a wedding dress down to her ankles.

And behind the minister, stuck in the grass not far back, a sign that said 50 Yard Line: Hook Up And Go.

Dee smiled. A paratrooper sign, all right. Six of them, three on each side of an aisle in front of the minister, Jake and Dummy and some others, dressed in their D-Day uniforms, crossing their rifles for the newlyweds to walk under, while the crowd around them cheered best wishes.

But not throwing rice. No way, not with the Longhorns needing to practice here in another hour or so. Plenty of cake, however, on a nearby table, the bride cutting one and passing slices around on paper plates. And another one, with Buck's name on it and two circles of candles around a red and white Navy flag in the center.

"You look embarrassed" said Dee. "Hell, you said let's do this on your birthday."

"You and Ashley" Buck replied. "You pricks get the number of candles right?"

"Ashley knew. And stop bitching, damn it, just because somebody cares."

Buck grinned. The first time Dee had seen him with that kind of look on his face. Grinning and saying thanks, you graduate and I'll have a cake for you, too, with a big time bonus stuck in the middle, so you can get the hell out of town and let me die in peace. Still grinning as Dee wandered away

A wedding and a birthday. On a cool October afternoon in Austin. Dee nodded as he watched the crowd. Seeing them mingle, eating cake and talking, maybe gossiping about this 50 yard line business. Seeing Arnie's uncle Wilbur among them, serving cake on paper plates.

Dee smiled. Wilbur, damn, he knows all about the 50 yard line, he was the one who turned the lights on back in August and saw them right here, Arnie and his future bride, naked as hell. No doubt pleased now, the way things turned out.

And Parker, at the edge of the crowd, with Rudy, the photographer, busy taking pictures. Parker wants some real gossip to write about, he should talk to Wilbur about the 50 yard line.

Dee started back to get a slice of cake, smiling at what Parker might dream up for tomorrow's paper, but he did not get there. He was stopped by the Chief, with one hand holding a duffel bag over his shoulders, heavy, Dee could tell, with rifle barrels sticking out of the top, holding a piece of cake in the other hand.

"Barbour sent me a message for you" said the Chief. "About some Bubba guy."

"Bubba? He sells barbecue in East Austin. A couple of cops tore down his door."

"He said tell you it was Holmes and Watson. Lomax is bragging about that, too."

"Damn, I have to tell you, at first I thought it was Abrams and Barbour who. . ."

"I know, they told me. But we're going to nail the bastards who really did it."

"Holmes and Watson, sure, if we can find out who they really are, but. . ."

"Don't worry, Barbour said Lomax wants him to help them, he' going to meet them soon. We'll know then, we'll have them by their balls."

The Chief set the duffle bag on the ground, munching on his cake, saying keep that to yourself, and don't tell Buck what Lomax said about your publisher, either, it's his birthday and that would ruin it, not like this crossed rifle show, that was great, but these damned things are heavy. Grunting as he picked up the bag and staggered away.

Dee looked down at the grass and shook his head. Right, and don't tell Ashley they're finally going to catch the bastards who tore up Bubba's place, not now, let Ashley stand over there with the newly weds, talking and laughing and rubbing his jaw, still trying to get over what his buddy Liebwitz did to his teeth.

Galloway had joined Parker and Rudy when Dee noticed them again. He looked at the line at the table, at everyone waiting for cake, with Buck and Ashley's daughter Amy serving as fast as they could. Hell, he might as well wait, maybe tease Galloway, see if he remembered what Amy looked like on the 50 yard line when they first saw her there.

He reached them just in time to hear Rudy say he had enough pictures, he was heading back to the office if anyone needed a ride. With Parker saying yes and Galloway saying no, he had to stick around and talk to Hopalong Tyrell when the Longhorns came out to practice.

"Tyrell, sure" said Dee. "Herman, a while ago, he mentioned some kind of odds. . ."

"Odds, no wonder" said Galloway "Tyrell wants to open a TV station in Austin."

"Why?" asked Dee. "So he can make speeches on it about sin and. . ."

"No" Galloway answered. "The West Texas folks who put him in office, they. . ."

"Last call" said Rudy. "I'm leaving."

"Go ahead, I'll walk" said Dee. "I want to hear what Tyrell is up to."

"They know LBJ has gotten rich off TV" said Galloway. "So they want Tyrell to see if he can get another one here. That's all. I suppose I'll write about it, hell, for sports it's been a dull week, anyway."

A dull week for sports, maybe, but not for crime. Dee said fine, we'll have a drink tonight at home and see what you find out, right now I'm going to have a piece of cake and chew on it, along with all the other crap I have to chew on, and that's a lot, considering what I've learned about East Austin in the last few days.

Once again he did not reach the table with the cakes. This time it was a dog, pulling at his trousers from behind. Dee turned around and looked. Another goddamn sniffing dog. This one only a puppy, on a leash, with a woman tugging on the leash and saying to the dog behave, damn it, this is the man I want to see.

"He's a wedding gift" said the woman. "From that paratrooper who can't talk."

"Dummy. I remember, he said he would give them a puppy, he said. . ."

"I'm holding him for Amy, we work together at the phone company."

"The phone company . . . so you. . ."

"I also work in your morgue. I have some folders to give you."

"The morgue? Then you must be Wanda, right? I recognize you now."

"I am, and you're that reporter Rudy talks about. He said give you these.."

"Rudy, sure . . . in the morgue, we were looking for some files, but. . ."

"They aren't originals. They're copies I made because of Charlie Black."

"Black. These are copies of the files he took? Wanda, let me hug you."

"He's a real asshole, Black, bossing me around, ordering me to find some files, so I figured if they're so important I would made copies while he wasn't looking."

She handed Dee a pair of folders, saying I don't need a hug but you could put a word in about the morgue, it's a mess and running it should be a full time job. Pulling on the dog's leash, saying I'm sorry if he keeps sniffing at your trousers, he's a mess, too, Amy should trade him in for a cat, they're nicer than dogs.

He looked at the folders as she walked away. One marked FCC, with a copy of a newspaper clipping, an AP story, three years old, reporting Congressman Lomax was now chair of the committee that approves TV licensing.

The other one, the East Austin election results from two years ago, the Democratic primary, showing a 99 per cent turnout, with 99 per cent voting for Lomax, the general election, 99 per cent again for Lomax.

The Mayor, too. Two years ago, 99 per cent for him in East Austin.

Dee shook his head. Like hell they had that kind of turnout, like hell they got all those votes, that had to be crooked, just as Trembley said. The Chief, show him these files, hell they have to tie in with Little Bob's dirty work.

Later. The Chief has disappeared. So keep it quite for now. Not a damned thing he could write about it, not with Black clamping down on what gets reported. And no point in telling Buck about these folders, either, that would really ruin his birthday.

His birthday, the crowd is gone and now he's picking up trash, Dee could see as he looked up from the folders and walked toward him. Buck, helping the stadium ground keepers stuff paper plates in a trash barrel and haul the tables away, clearing the field for the football team to practice.

"Here, I saved you some cake" said Buck.

"Cake. Thanks, I tried, but the line was. . ."

"Tastes sweet. Better than that dog sniffing at you."

"The dog . . . right . . . he's a wedding present, he. . ."

"That dog at Hattie's, that old man he was sniffing for, before he dropped dead."

"So what are you trying to tell me, Buck?"

"Sniffing dogs. Sniffing just like you, goddamn it. One of these days you'll sniff a pile of shit and get us all fired."

Buck grunted and said come along, I'll give you a ride back to the office. Dee followed, glancing down at the folders in his hand, copies of the files Black grabbed from the morgue. A pile of shit? Maybe, maybe not.

Sniffing dogs. Sniffing, hell, find out why Black wants those files kept secret, one of these dogs may start biting, too.

LULU'S LAST HEADLINE

PROFESSOR EASTMAN GOT UP FROM HIS DESK, WALKED TO A book case, glanced inside a thick red volume, came back and sat down, reading the footnotes Dee had added to his rewrite of the Juneteenth paper.

While Dee stared at the picture of Eastman's dead wife, with her watch still hanging there, wondering again how he could have been so wrong about a couple of policemen trying to steal it.

"I have verified your sources, Mister Dee. Excellent research this time."

"Research . . . well . . . yes, my first stab, you said it was too much like journalism."

"Journalism. Have you thought about graduate school?"

"With my grades? Working full time, I've barely. . ."

"I understand. But suppose this paper is published."

"Published? Who would. . ."

"One of the Texas history journals. How would you feel then?"

"About graduate school, you mean? I don't know, I. . ."

"You should think ahead. There is no future for you in journalism, Dee. Television will make your kind of reporting obsolete."

Speaking softly, Professor Eastman had not looked up from the Juneteenth paper, thumbing through its pages and nodding. Dee looked on, silent. Graduate school? No way. But what Eastman had just said about the future . . . hell, maybe. . .

"Poison" said Eastman. "I expect it will prove to be a terrible addiction, television."

"I don't watch TV, sir. I don't have time, I. . ."

"Once pictures replace words, everything will change. In a way, it already has."

"Newspaper work, you said that would. . ."

"The fear of an atomic war, what is a natural reaction to that, Dee?"

"I don't know . . . build a bomb shelter, I guess. . ."

"No. People buy things. More clothes, more phonograph records, more junk, anything to ward off the fear of annihilation. Television plays right into that."

Dee watched as Eastman looked down at his wife's picture. Television. What had Buck called it? Trash, nothing but Lucille Ball crap? Whatever, it was obvious Eastman had more on his mind than Lucille Ball as he looked up at Dee and went on talking.

"You should watch the commercials some time."

"The commercials, professor? They. . ."

"They show how happy people are when they buy things. That's a lie, of course, but it works." Eastman shook his head as he spoke, then got up from his desk and walked to a window, looking out at the campus, talking now with his back to Dee.

"Commercials, Dee. That's how you get rich if you own a TV station."

"Like Senator Johnson, you mean."

"My wife" said Eastman. "Do you remember what Johnson told her?"

"About the election, you said she. . ."

"The election, it's all about television, Johnson told her."

"Yessir, I saw him myself, I was going to ask him what he meant by that."

"And did he tell you?"

"No . . . we were interrupted . . . by a seeing eye dog, professor, it. . ."

Eastman turned and stared at Dee, his face showing no expression at all. No wonder, and no way to explain it to him, that night when LBJ was about to talk, when that blind man came into Hattie's and died in Ginger's arms, hell, tell Eastman about that and he'll throw that Juneteenth paper in the wastebasket and maybe worse, maybe. . .

Wrong again.

"That dog" said Eastman. "He was quite fond of that dog."

"You knew about that? Professor, how did you. . ."

"Let's just say an associate told me, and let it go at that."

"Then you must know he left the dog to her . . . to Hattie . . . and left her. . ."

"He also left a great deal of money to the University, Dee."

"Really? I guess there will be a story about that in the paper . . . but not about who he left the dog to, they wouldn't publish that."

Dee tried to laugh as he said that, relieved, in a way, that Eastman somehow knew what had happened at Hattie's, relieved his Juneteenth paper was not headed for the wastebasket. But Eastman was not even smiling as he replied.

"Why not? Your paper has endorsed Congressman Lomax, has it not?"

"The publisher, Black, yes he did that, but. . ."

"Lomax is as crooked as they come. He takes bribes, you know."

"No, I didn't, I. . ."

"Your paper can endorse Lomax, but not even mention a whorehouse madam, too?"

Eastman sat down and leaned forward, took his wife's watch from her picture and started winding it. Slowly, looking at the picture. While Dee watched and nodded. What Eastman had just said, about money, about the paper, about Lomax taking bribes, about getting rich if you own a TV station, damn, it's starting to add up.

Throw in what's in those files Black lifted from the morgue, that fifty thousand dollars he withdrew from the paper's operating budget, what the Chief said about the mayor, it's starting to added up, all right.

To something crooked as hell. With a lot of dirty money under the table, and their fingerprints all over it, Black and Lomax and the Mayor, all three of those bastards in it together.

"Professor, I think I can guess now what Senator Johnson had in mind."

"You mean when he told my wife this election is all about television."

"If I'm right you'll know soon enough. Maybe not in the paper but. . ."

"You should forget the paper. Think about your future."

Eastman was still looking at his wife's picture, his mind no doubt on her, when Dee thanked him for the advice and left, heading downtown to work. Think about his future? There may not be any future in what he's about to do.

By the time the bus had reached his stop downtown Dee had figured out how to let Buck and Ashley in on it, step by step and word for word the crooked scheme he had uncovered.

All right, here's how it must be going down: Black gives fifty thousand to Lomax, the Mayor steals money from the car raffle to add to that, Lomax uses the money to get elected again, and then sees to it they get a license for a TV station.

And Black and the Mayor get rich as hell. Together. Bribing their way to a fortune. That has to be what Senator Johnson meant when he told Eastman's wife this election is all about television.

But walking up the hill to the office he was not so sure they would believe it. Even when he showed them the files Black had swiped. Another of your goddamn hunches, Buck will say. And Ashley, he'll say what you've got proves nothing.

Wrong again. This time, wrong as hell. They were in Buck's office, with the door open. When he asked if he could see them, he could tell by the look on their faces something bad had happened, and they were not about to let him tell them anything.

"You'll be living all alone now, Phil" said Ashley.

"Maybe now you can get some sleep" said Buck.

"Living alone? Sleep?" said Dee. "What are you talking about?"

"Galloway and Parker" said Ashley.

"Black just fired them both" said Buck.

"He fired them?" Dee replied. "That bastard fired them? What for?" As he spoke, raising his voice in anger, Ashley stepped behind him and closed the door, saying "Careful, Black's on a rampage, he may can you too if he hears you."

"He read Galloway's column this morning" said Buck. "That's what did it."

"But damn it, Black never reads the paper" said Dee, lowering his voice.

"Black won a golf tournament some place" said Ashley. "So. . ."

"We think he figured Galloway would be writing about that" said Buck.

"So he fired him because he didn't write about his damn golf game?"

No answer. Buck was silent for a moment, then sat down at his desk, shaking his head, saying "Maybe it's my fault, Galloway getting fired. I should have told him Black ruled politics is off limits, but hell, I never dreamed. . ."

"Politics? Jack wrote something about politics?" Dee asked.

"Not much, a couple of sentences about Congressman Lomax" said Ashley.

"Lomax and what it costs to get a TV license" said Buck.

"Lomax" said Dee. "Sure, Black's buddy, he. . ."

"Parker, dumb, but he tried to talk him out of firing Galloway" said Buck.

"So he fired Parker, too, half an hour ago" said Ashley.

"They're still here, see them, they'll fill you in" said Buck,

"That sonofabitch will pay for this" Dee muttered as he left the office. With Buck and Ashley shaking their heads, no doubt still trying to swallow what had happened. And no doubt unaware he meant it.

As for Galloway, he would not even listen when Dee started to tell him what he planned to do. He went on packing a box of papers from his desk, looking up and smiling in a fatherly kind of way.

"Don't do anything stupid, Phil" he said. "Finish school, get your degree."

"Maybe. But Black, what the hell did you write that pissed him off?"

"Remember I said I was going to write a column about Hopalong Tyrell?"

"That football player, sure, something about his trying to get a TV license. . ."

"For the people he represents from West Texas, they asked him to do it."

"A TV license, sure, I think I can guess why Black. . ."

"This is what he was raising hell about, the part I've circled with a grease pencil" said Galloway, reaching across his desk for a copy of the morning paper, turning to the sports page and pointing to his column. Dee nodded as he read that part:

When I asked him how it was going, Tyrell said "Well, I've learned a license will cost $50,000 and they will have to deal with a Congressman named Lomax, but my folks back home say it's not supposed to cost a penny and they haven't made up their minds yet." So we moved on to talk about this week's game.

"No wonder he fired you" said Dee. "He's covering for Lomax."

"Well, to hell with it" said Galloway. "I've got a better job already."

"Already? Where?"

"Houston. The Post. One call, and they want me there tomorrow."

"What about Parker? I understand he. . ."

"He's downstairs getting his two week's severance pay" said Galloway. As he spoke he pointed to the elevator and Dee turned to see Parker coming into the city room, going to his desk, picking up a box he had packed and coming toward them.

"Tough shit" said Parker. "You sure as hell can't argue with Black."

"No" said Dee. "But I'm going to expose that crooked bastard."

"Forget it" said Parker. "Get your degree, finish college first."

"That's what I told him" said Galloway. "Ready to go, Steve?"

"Ready" said Parker. "Look, Phil, the rent's paid up for a month, so. . ."

"You're leaving with Jack?" asked Dee. "Both of you, right now?

"Going to Houston" said Parker. "Maybe I can get a job there, too."

"I understand they need a good amusements editor" said Galloway.

"If not, I may head for Hollywood" said Parker. "Be a press agent."

"Press agent?" Dee responded. "Steve, you can't. . ."

"You bet" said Parker, laughing. "Meredith Ogletree, you watch, she's going to be famous with that screaming shit. And we put her in the movies, didn't we? She's going to need a damned good press agent."

Parker was still laughing as the three shook hands and hugged each other farewell, with Galloway and Parker saying they would come back when he graduates, and get drunk as hell and celebrate at Hattie's but not now, they're heading for Houston.

The city room was almost silent, some of them shaking hands with Galloway and Parker as they headed for the elevator, some of them watching Dee as he headed for the men's room, where he washed his face and lingered, nodding and cursing.

When he returned Ashley was back at his desk, back at work, holding his telephone in one hand, marking copy with the other hand. Dee stood in front of him, waiting until he had finished on the phone. Waiting to make his next move.

"So what do you want?" asked Ashley. "You want Parker's old job?"

"No" said Dee. "I'll stick with the police beat."

"Really? Not the amusements section? You seemed to like that shit when you two made fun of that Ogletree woman." Ashley went back to marking copy, while Dee waited until he looked up again.

"All right" said Ashley. "What is it you want?"

"I will have a front page story for you tomorrow" said Dee.

"Really? What about?"

"They're raffling off that Cadillac at noon, and. . ."

"So what? That's not front page new, that's not even. . ."

"You want to know who broke into Bubba's, don't you?"

"Hell yes, but what does that have to do with this raffle?"

"You'll see tomorrow, just keep the front page open." Dee walked away then, hearing Ashley mumble "Dee, you're a goddamn basket case, that raffle doesn't have crap to do with the police beat and you know it."

A basket case. Maybe. But tomorrow, when they raffle off that Cadillac, when the Chief arrests the Mayor for stealing all the ticket money, for hiring the goons who broke into Bubba's, when he brings that story in, Ashley will change his tune.

Right, when he ties Lomax and the Mayor to that crooked bastard Black they'll both change their tunes, Buck and Ashley, both of them, they'll see what Black's been up to, bribing Lomax. And let the chips fall where they may.

The street in front of City Hall was blocked off and crowded, at least a thousand people waiting in the sunshine to see who would drive the Cadillac away, as Dee inched his way forward, trying to get a better view of the platform with the car on it and the top down and the big sign behind it saying Win This Car All Proceeds Go To Charity.

As he got closer he could see the officials standing next to the car, the Mayor, Little Bob, in front of a microphone, and behind him the Chief of Police and the City Attorney, along with some others he did not know. And next to the Mayor a blindfolded woman in front of a huge glass jar, ready to draw out the winning ticket stub.

Dee looked at his watch as the Mayor tapped the microphone to see if the loudspeaker was working. Exactly noon. Right, and in five minutes, as soon as that woman pulls out the winning number and Little Bob hands off the keys to the Cadillac the Chief will slap handcuffs on him. So much for All Proceeds Go to Charity.

"You folks bought that whole big jar full of tickets" said Little Bob and the crowd cheered. "Enough to take care of all the Boy Scouts in Austin." Again the crowd cheered. "And Mildred here, she's a clerk from upstairs we grabbed at random, she's gonna reach in there now and find out who won this big old Cadillac."

The crowd went on cheering as Mildred, whoever she was, held one hand over her blindfold and stuck the other in the jar, fumbling around among thousands of tickets, then pulling one out of the pile and holding it out so Little Bob could take it, look at it, keep the crowd in suspense for another moment, and then read the number out loud.

"Number one nine three five" Little Bob announced as the crowd became silent. He paused for a moment, waiting. "One nine three five" he repeated. "Ain't anybody out there got that number?"

One nine three five.

Nineteen thirty five.

The year he was born.

Dee reached in his wallet, searching for the raffle ticket he had won two months ago, in that poker game with the printers, when Arnie had thrown it in the pot. Damn, no way, impossible, but that's what he remembered, laughing about the number on it matching the year he was born.

When he found it stuck behind his driver's license he looked at the ticket again and again, rubbing his eyes to be sure. One nine three five, all right. Stunned, unable to believe his luck, forgetting what he had come there to cover, he moved forward, up the platform ramp, and without a word held the ticket up so Little Bob could see it.

"We have a winner" said Little Bob after he looked at the ticket. It was obvious the Mayor did not recognize him, even after all their encounters. Good, that will make it easier, Dee surmised, as he slowly came to his senses and remembered what he was there for. To cover Little Bob's downfall.

The crowd cheered and went on cheering as Little Bob handed Dee the keys to the Cadillac and patted him on the back, then asked, talking into the microphone, "What's your name, son, and what do you do here in Austin?"

"Phillip Dee. I work for the paper."

"His name is Phillip Dee and he works for the paper" said Little Bob over the loudspeaker, still working the crowd. "Well, son, now you can deliver your papers in this big old Cadillac."

As the crowd began to disperse Little Bob turned away from the microphone and walked away, evidently heading back to his office. Dee followed, watching the City Attorney grab him by the shoulder and guide him behind the sign, where the Police Chief was waiting with his handcuffs.

"I'm sorry, but you're under arrest, Mister Mayor" said the Chief.

"What?" shouted Little Bob. "What in hell's going on here?"

"For stealing all the profits from this raffle" the Chief replied.

"Grand larceny" said the City Attorney.

Right on cue, Rudy stepped in front of Dee with his Speed Graphic and shot a picture of the Chief handcuffing the Mayor. And then a second picture of the Chief and the City Attorney wrestling with Little Bob as they pushed him through a doorway into City Hall.

"Good work" Dee said to Rudy.

"Right" Rudy replied. "That second one, that's Life Magazine shit."

As they spoke the City Attorney came rushing out of the doorway, out of breath and heading for Dee, saying "I almost forgot, you can't drive that car yet, I have the title and it's evidence for the jury when we try the Mayor."

"So you want the keys, do you?" asked Dee.

"Just a technicality. It's your car, tax free, but you'll have to wait."

"I can wait, just keep it hidden, so no one throws rocks at it."

"Because of the Mayor, right. That's why we arrested him behind this sign."

"To keep that hidden? So the crowd couldn't see that crooked bastard being. . ."

"Look, Dee, how we were going to handle this, why we wanted to keep it from the crowd, I explained that to your bosses in advance. Go argue with them, not me, they're right over there by that statue."

Dee turned and saw them, Buck and Ashley, both of them standing next to the statue of some Texan who died at the Alamo. His bosses, right, but what were they doing here? He'd mentioned the raffle to Ashley and he'd said he would have a front page story for him, sure, but. . .

"What you told me, we decided to see for ourselves" said Ashley.

"Looks like one of your damned hunches was finally right" said Buck.

"It wasn't a hunch" said Dee. "I knew, and I know a lot more."

"More? What else?" Ashley asked.

"Buck, you remember that fifty thousand dollar check Black wrote?"

"I remember" said Buck. "So what?"

"Black, he's in it with Little Bob, they're bribing Lomax together to. . ."

"Bullshit" said Buck. "Black and the Mayor hate each other."

"LBJ" Dee replied. "Remember he said this election is all about TV?"

"Hell yes, I remember" said Buck. "I saw him this morning and. . ."

"Black and Little Bob, they're in it together, even if they hate each other" said Dee. "Bribing Lomax to get a TV license, that's why Black fired Galloway, he's covering for Lomax, Buck, he's after a television station, that's what LBJ meant when he. . ."

"More of your bullshit" said Buck, shaking his head. "Senator Johnson told me himself this morning. You want to know what he meant? He meant this is the first time we'll see how TV can change the outcome of an election, that's all."

With that, Buck turned to Ashley and said "Amos, you'll have to write this story about the Mayor's arrest."

"Me? This should be Phil's story, Buck, he. . ."

"Dee can't, because he won that car, that's news by itself" said Buck.

"Right, I can see what you. . ."

"How he managed to win it I don't know, but we'll stick that some place else, just don't mention him in your story about this arrest."

"All right" said Ashley. "I'll find out what I can from the Chief and. . ."

"And not a word about what Little Bob stole the money for, not yet."

"Right, I know, and not a word about Lomax, even if. . ."

"I'll find the City Attorney and see what he knows" said Buck. "Whatever, it's front page, of course. With one of those pictures Rudy took, damned big. We'll just have to wait and see how Black wants to handle it."

"Damn" said Ashley. "A hell of a time for him to be out of town."

They went into City Hall, leaving Dee standing next to the statue. A Texan killed at the Alamo, it could be worse. It's not the Alamo for him, but it might as well be. He has a car he can't drive, a front page story he can't write, and a managing editor who thinks he's all bullshit.

Right, so to hell with it. Stick to the Blotter. No more scoops. Stay out of trouble. Let them see how Black wants to handle it. No telling what that crooked bastard will say.

The biggest local story in years and Dee, who had made it happen, could not even talk about it. And not a word about how the paper would handle it, either, not even a hint from Buck that it had happened. But they knew in the city room, half of them huddled around a portable radio, some of them shouting and patting each other on the back as they listened to the radio report of Little Bob's arrest.

Dee sat at his desk, shaking his head. Talking on the telephone and working the police beat. A robbery at a bookstore across from the University, no suspect apprehended. A car crash in South Austin, two people in the hospital. All quiet at the local precinct, and so far nothing at all in East Austin.

As Dee finished with the telephone he looked up to see Lulu standing in front of his desk. Lulu, wearing a tight red dress, with her hands on her hips, smiling, no doubt ready for another exercise in double entendres. Fine. A bit of relief, perhaps, from the crap he's been getting from Buck.

"They said on the radio you won that Cadillac, Phil."

"Really. Did they tell you why I can't drive it yet?"

"I didn't hear, but I expect you'll give me a ride when you get it."

"Whatever you say, Lulu."

"At night, with the top down, that's the best time for a ride."

"At night, you bet."

"In the back seat, where there's a lot of room, that's the best place for a ride."

With that she walked away, toward the ring. Then she stopped, turned half way around, looked back at Dee and winked. A wink, what the hell could that mean? No way to know, and no time to guess, not with Ashley sitting down in the chair next to his desk. Ashley, with a look on his face that spelled disgust.

"I've got a problem with this story I'm supposed to write" said Ashley.

"A problem with the Mayor stealing money. My, my."

"A problem with the Mayor bribing voters in East Austin."

"East Austin. You took me out there to meet Bubba, remember?"

"I wish to hell I'd never heard of East Austin."

"Juneteenth, that's how the Blotter got started. Remember?"

"I remember, but. . ."

"Somebody broke down Bubba's door, remember?"

"I remember. But this damned story about the mayor, I. . ."

"I can't help you with that, Amos. Buck said so."

Ashley did not reply. Staring down at the floor, he said nothing for a moment or two. Maybe trying to get his mind clear about something, Dee could not tell. At least he's not winking. He's not as crazy as Lulu, he's. . .

"It's Buck" said Ashley. "I've never seen him so uncertain."

"Uncertain? Hell, he. . ."

"He can't make up his mind how to play this story about the mayor."

"Because it's politics? Because. . ."

"Because Black said he'd write all the political stories himself."

"Sure, and Buck agreed to that, I know, so what's the problem?"

"Black, he's in Kansas, and Buck has not been able to contact him."

"And Buck can't decide what to do with the mayor's story, right?"

"Right. Maybe you can help him make up his mind."

"What is it, five hours to press time? How could I help?"

"What put you on to the mayor in the first place? That might. . ."

"Hattie. She figured it out, she told the police chief and. . ."

"Your phone's ringing. God ahead, answer it, we've got time."

Ashley watched as Dee answered the phone, started writing some notes, and then wadded up the notes and tossed them in a wastebasket. He nodded several times as he spoke but his voice was too soft for Ashley to hear what he was saying. Until the last thing he said before he hung up the phone.

"The parking lot in five minutes, we'll be there, both of us" said Dee.

"Who was that?" asked Ashley. "What's this about the parking lot?"

"You want to know who broke down Bubba's door?"

"Sure, but who. . ."

"You want to know how to get Buck to make up his mind?"

"Yes, of course, but. . ."

"You want to know how to square things with East Austin?"

"East Austin, all right, but. . ."

"You want to know how to put that bastard Black in jail?"

"Black? I'm not. . ."

"That call was one hell of a break, Amos. If I'm right, all you want to know is waiting down there in the parking lot. Let's go see."

There they were, just as she said they would be, Debbie Decker standing next to that roadster with the rumble seat, her arm around Fritz Bordon, the tall policeman she just now said she's engaged to, Bordon not in uniform, wearing a suit and tie, holding a couple of ledgers as Dee approached them with Ashley following behind.

Dee introduced Ashley and then spoke directly to Bordon.

"Last time we met was at the Tavern" said Dee. "A lot has happened since then."

"A lot" said Bordon. "Jody and me, we're not working anymore for Lomax."

"Holmes and Watson?" asked Dee. "You used those names, right?"

"Sure, we used all kinds of fake names in East Austin."

"Debbie said you quit this morning, after Lomax. . ."

"After we watched him beat up his Negro mistress. He damned near killed her."

"He had a mistress? A colored mistress? Lomax?"

"She's in the hospital. Broken jaw, fractured ribs, on oxygen."

"Your buddy, Bruce Jody, he saw it too? Where is he now?"

"Gone. We've both turned in out badges. Quit the force. We. . ."

"Wait" said Ashley, stepping in front of Dee, standing in front of Bordon, shaking his head. "You two, Bordon and Jody, right? You were the ones who broke down the door at Bubba's place on Rosewood? You tore down his American flag, right off the wall, you. . ."

"That place on Rosewood? Sure, that could have been us, we. . ."

"Could have been? What does that mean?"

"I don't even remember. We were drunk most of the time."

"Bubba had broken bones, did you know that?"

"Look, we were a couple of rotten apples, I admit it" said Bordon. "Hell, selling out to Lomax we were rotten, all right, but Debbie here, she turned us around, she got us to sober up and join her church and start behaving. Lomax beating up his woman, that was just the last straw. I've brought these ledgers to. . ."

"He's brought these ledgers to atone for their sins" said Debbie.

"These ledgers, what's in them?" asked Ashley.

"All of the records Lomax kept, bribes, payoffs, everything" Bordon answered.

"Debbie, you told me on the phone it's enough to put Lomax in jail" said Dee.

"Your publisher, too" she replied. "Along with the Mayor."

"Damn" Ashley muttered. "These ledgers, Bordon, how did you get them?"

"Last night, Lomax told me to hide them, with election day coming up he wanted them moved to a safe place. I might have done it, too, but this morning. . ."

"This morning you saw what Lomax did to his woman" said Dee.

"All right" said Ashley. "I've heard enough. Let's go, all four of us, up to the managing editor's office with these ledgers. We'll see what he says."

"I'll pray he does the right thing" said Debbie. "I will pray for him."

"No Debbie, it's me you should pray for" said Dee as they walked from the parking lot to the city room elevator. "With the way Buck's been kicking my butt, when we show him these ledgers he may send me off to sweep the floors in that church of yours."

Buck was staring at the Navy pictures on his wall, with his

back to the door of his office, talking to himself, out loud, cursing, when they opened the door and entered, all four of them, as quiet as they could be, hearing what he was muttering.

"I'm a goddamn coward. I've let that bastard Black turn me into a coward."

"Not a coward. An A plus managing editor" said Dee from behind him.

Buck turned around when he heard Dee's voice. As he did he saw the rest of them, Ashley with two people he had never seen before. "Who are you?" he asked. "What are you doing in my office?"

"I brought them" said Dee. "You should look at what they have."

Bordon placed the ledgers on Buck's desk, two volumes side by side, then opened one of them and began to talk. "This one has a separate code" he said. "When I give you the code you'll see it shows how the Mayor's been bribing Lomax to stay in office."

Buck listened, wrote some notes as Bordon gave him the code, then started to groan. "It's sure as hell up to date" he said. "That entry yesterday, that's the forty thousand dollars Little Bob stole from raffling off that Cadillac Dee won."

"Two years ago it was a yacht" said Bordon. "See that entry, right there?"

"No wonder the Mayor always carries East Austin" said Buck.

"Close to a hundred per cent. Lomax pockets the money, the Mayor gets elected."

"How does he do it? How does he get all these people to vote for Little Bob?"

"Simple, as simple as fried chicken" said Bordon. "It's not how they vote that counts. It's how their votes get counted."

Buck watched as Bordon flipped through the pages of the ledger, explaining how Lomax had a Negro mistress who kept the records for him, how the different columns showed the names of voters, the date they voted, how they voted, and how their vote was actually recorded. Buck nodded, then turned the pages, looking for a certain name.

"This woman" he muttered. "She was our maid. She died three years ago."

"But she's voted in two elections since then" said Bordon as he looked at the entry Buck was pointing to. "Hell, all the people buried in the East Side cemetery, they all vote for Little Bob. You can match the voting records with the tombstones."

Buck and Bordon both turned to look at Dee when they heard his voice from the other side of the room. "Wait" said Dee. "His mistress kept those records for him? So why did Lomax beat her up so bad she's in the hospital?"

"Lomax beat her?" asked Buck.

"Corina Whipple" said Bordon. "Here, in this other ledger, I'll show you why."

The second ledger contains the names of people Lomax has been involved with in a number of crooked schemes, Bordon explained. Money back and forth, in Washington and Texas, much of it spelled out in codes he had no knowledge of. "Except for this one" he said. "A week ago and it's not coded at all. You can see for yourself."

Buck read it, shaking his head. Then he read it again, this time out loud, so everyone in the room could hear it.

"Fifty thousand dollars from Charlie Black, for issue of TV station license."

"That's a crime" said Ashley. "You can't sell a TV license, it's not. . ."

"It's a crime, all right" said Buck. "So why did she write it that way?"

"I don't know" Bordon answered. "She could have said it was a campaign contribution, that would have made it legal. Maybe she was being snotty."

"This entry" said Buck. "This is the deposit receipt, right?"

"Right" said Bordon. "Fifty thousand, right there in his account."

"Lomax, he just saw it today?" asked Dee. "This morning, what she had written?"

"This morning, that's when he broke her jaw and worked her over."

"That's when Fritz decided to show these ledgers to the paper" said Debbie, who had stood in the corner silent while everyone else talked.

"I need to keep them" said Bordon. "As long as Lomax knows I have them he won't come after me."

"I understand" said Buck. "We'll have you on your way in a few minutes."

Turning to Ashley, he said "I've made up my mind, Amos. Get Rudy, he can take some pictures of these pages, especially the ones that mention Charlie Black."

"What about Black?" asked Ashley. "When will he be back?"

"Tomorrow evening. I called the airport, that's what they told me."

"The story about the mayor" said Ashley. "You want me to. . ."

"I want you to write it. "You know what to say. Little Bob goes to jail."

"I still say that's Dee's story" said Ashley.

"No" said Buck. "I've got something else for him. Black and Lomax."

"You're going after them?" asked Dee. "Black, too, in tonight's edition?"

"On the front page. And you're going to write the story, young man."

"Wait" said Ashley.

"Wait, hell, let's see if Dee can unseat this bastard Lomax."

"Buck, damn it" said Ashley. "You know what that means?"

The room was dead silent, all of them waiting to hear Buck's answer, while Rudy took pictures and Buck, with a smile on his face, reached in a cabinet behind his desk and brought out a bottle of whiskey and some glasses, pouring only three, as if he knew Debbie and Bordon would decline.

"Damn right I know" he said. "It means tomorrow night we'll be unemployed."

"Black, he'll fire you for writing about him?" asked Bordon. "Sure, I see. . ."

"He will" said Ashley.

"Then it's bottoms up" said Dee, reaching for one of the glasses.

"Right" said Ashley, sipping slowly. "I agree, Buck, we have no choice."

"Hell" said Buck. "You're not a real newspaperman unless you've been fired at least once." And then, turning to Dee, he started laughing, saying "You thought I would fire you some day. Maybe I should have, before you brought all this on."

"Maybe" said Dee. "Either way it's two weeks severance pay, right?"

"Tomorrow" said Buck. "We all show up so Black can fire us."

"Omar, I'm sorry" said Debbie. "We didn't mean for this to happen."

"Don't worry about it" said Dee, motioning to Debbie and Bordon that he would guide them to the elevator, telling her things are fine, it may take a miracle but now he can concentrate on getting a degree, hearing her say she believes in miracles as he hugged her goodbye.

And then Ashley, as Dee sat down and started typing.

"Do you believe in miracles, Phil?"

"Miracles? I don't know, Debbie said. . ."

"You should. Getting the goods on Black this way, it's a miracle, by damn, no matter what happens next."

Twenty four hours later Dee sat at his desk, looking at the morning edition, looking at his byline under a six column headline, reading the story he had written about Black and Lomax colluding in a crime, looking at his watch, once again calculating how long it would take Black to get to the city room now that his plane has landed.

When he stepped out of the elevator Black was not alone. His secretary was behind him, and Lomax was right behind her. Dee realized it was the first time he had seen the Congressman that close. Six feet six and he looked bigger than that. Black and Lomax were waving copies of the morning paper, looking angry enough to kill.

They walked past Dee and faced the city room staff. "These pictures from some ledger, they're forgeries. Who is responsible for this?" asked Black, pointing to the story about himself and Lomax, almost snarling. Two or three raised their hands at once, then slowly all the others, until everyone had a hand up.

"My ass" yelled Black. "Which one of you bastards wrote this?"

"I did" said Dee. "That's my byline."

"I helped him write it" said Ashley, standing in the hallway to Buck's office.

"And I told him to" said Buck behind him. "We're all guilty. All three of us."

"And by God then you're all fired" said Black, having spun around when he first heard Dee's voice behind him. Fine. Everything right on schedule. Severance pay guaranteed now. So go to the finance office and collect it. Before this monster Lomax beats someone to death, since he looks like he's ready to do just that.

"That little prick, that's Dee, is it?" yelled Lomax.

"That's him" said Black. And then, to his secretary he barked "Hildegarde, are you ready to take dictation? I'm going to tell you what to write for tomorrow's paper. So listen to what I tell you."

And to Lulu, standing in front of the ring: "I want a six column headline on what she writes, top of the front page, got it?"

And back to Lomax: "We'll stick a two column picture next to it, a paste-up, showing Dee shaking your hand and apologizing."

Dee cringed when he heard that. Apologizing to Lomax. But what the hell, it's Black's paper, he can do whatever he pleases.

Except he can't satisfy Lomax with a paste-up of Dee apologizing.

"No, damn it" said Lomax. "That's not enough."

"All right" said Black. "Then we'll. . ."

"This little prick, the way he tried to screw me, I'd like to castrate the bastard."

"By God, that's a good idea" said Black. "Castrate him."

"Castrate him" said Lomax. "Chop off his dong."

"Castrate him, right" said Black. "So he'll never screw anybody again. Never."

Dee had slipped away as Black and Lomax ranted on. Heading for the elevator, he looked back and saw Black's secretary, sitting at the desk he had just vacated. Starting to type while looking at the notes in her stenographic pad. Every word Black had uttered.

When he got to the elevator, Back and Ashley were waiting. "Sounds like Black needs to hire a surgeon" said Buck, laughing as the elevator door closed. "Don't worry, Phil" said Ashley. "We'll hold your hands when they operate on you."

At three o'clock in the morning, they sat side by side at Hattie's bar. Buck and Ashley, with Dee in the middle. Looking at the latest edition of the paper, Black's revenge for the story exposing his crooked arrangement with Lomax.

"Might as well kiss off the primary now" said Ashley.

"Lomax" said Dee. "He gets endorsed by Black, he's in."

"And Black get his TV station" said Buck.

"Maybe so" said Ashley. "But he won't win any prizes for page layout."

"You're right" said Dee. "That paste-up picture of me shaking hands with Lomax. It looks like some damned midget reaching up to say hello."

"A midget" muttered Buck. "So you're really going to join the Army, are you?"

"I am. I don't have a job anymore, all I have is severance pay."

"And college" said Ashley. "What about that?"

"I can finish with correspondence courses. Hell, you two, you'll have other jobs by noon tomorrow, right? As soon as you make some calls you will. . ."

"True" said Buck. "But the real winner is. . ."

"Lulu" said Ashley.

"Who is Lulu?" asked Hattie as she brought them another round of drinks.

"Lulu's the one who wrote that headline" said Buck, pointing to the paper, to the six column headline next to the paste-up picture of Dee:

BLACK SAYS CASTRATED DEE CAN'T EVER DO IT AGAIN

"That headline" said Hattie, laughing. "Is it true?"

"Don't know" said Buck. "I think that depends on what it means."

"Lomax said it meant chop off his dong" said Ashley.

"Lomax?" said Hattie. "He's the one who should get that kind of. . ."

"Wait" said Buck, reaching in his wallet and placing a ten dollar bill on the counter, saying "Here, I'll bet this much it's not true, no matter what it means. "

"Ten more" said Ashley. "Ten more says it's not true."

"That's twenty dollars" said Dee. "Where's Ginger?"

"There she is" said Hattie. "Coming down the stairs."

"All right, by damn" said Dee. "Let's take this twenty and see if it's true."

With that he walked to the stairs, towards Ginger. While the others laughed again at the headline. Lulu's last headline. With Dee looking back and smiling, saying "This won't take long, so wait here and I'll let you know if it's true."

"My, my" said Hattie, also nodding and smiling. "I don't think it's true, either, but if it is, remember, no refunds."

THE HOUSE ON HAUNTED HILL

"HELL NO, THAT'S NOT TRUE. IT NEVER WAS" SAID DEE, looking up at the front page in the frame on Herman's wall. Shaking his head once more time upon seeing Lulu's last headline.

"That page is nearly five years old" said Herman. "But I still laugh every time I look at it."

"Lulu" said Dee. "I wonder whatever happened to her."

"Lulu? I heard she's teaching journalism at some university."

"And Lomax keeps getting elected."

"Sure, because Black keeps endorsing him."

"Black and Lomax. A marriage made in hell, Herman."

"The rumor is Black wants to own a chain of TV stations, not just one."

"Damn, he's already rich, he. . ."

"Lomax would have to approve it. That's why Black keeps endorsing him."

"Well, to hell with both of them, Herman. I'm on my way."

Dee stood up, straightened his uniform, gave Herman a farewell handshake, and walked out to his car.

When he got to his car he saw the lady who had complained about Texas drinking laws when she came into Herman's to order a bottle of Scotch. She was standing in front of the theater, holding a briefcase, evidently waiting for a taxi.

"Where are you headed?" he asked.

"The state Capitol area" she answered.

"So am I" he said. "If you like I can give you a lift."

As she got in the car she glanced at the theater sign labeled Coming Attractions and read the title out loud. "The House on

Haunted Hill" she said. "The people in the hotel bar seemed to be excited about it."

"Really? Did they tell you why?"

"I believe there's a lady from Austin in it. Meredith somebody."

"Meredith Ogletree, sure. She's sort of a local movie star."

"I understand that's a horror movie. She stars in horror movies?"

"You might say that. All she ever does is scream."

"You've seen her movies, have you?"

"Sure, you might even say I helped her get started."

"Horror movies" she muttered. "Where I work, every day is another damned horror movie."

"Really? So where is that?"

"I work in Washington" she said.

"Washington? You have a government job?"

"More or less" she answered.

"So do I" said Dee, laughing. "I guess you'd say the Army is a government job."

She did not reply. Dee shrugged his shoulders and continued to look straight ahead as he drove toward the Capitol. He could see the lights had gone on. Nice, with all the different colors lighting up the dome. Nice, all right, but in its own way, eerie, too.

"That movie" he said. "The House on Haunted Hill. You know, ma'am, that could be a movie about the Capitol."

No reply.

"A lot of ghosts might be prowling the hallways there."

Again, no reply.

"Davy Crockett, Jim Bowie, all the folks who died at the Alamo."

Still no reply.

"Yes, ma'am, The House on Haunted Hill."

His passenger remained silent as Dee stopped at a traffic light half way to the Capitol. She was fumbling in her brief case for something.

"When I came into that liquor store this afternoon I noticed you are in the Eighty Second Airborne Division" she said. "That says Dee on your nameplate. So you are Lieutenant Dee, I take it."

"Yes, ma'am, Lieutenant Phillip Dee."

"Where is your next assignment?"

"Germany. Soon as I get this car back to Bragg, I. . ."

"You're going in the wrong direction."

"No, this is the way to the Capitol, you can see it. . ."

"I'm not talking about your driving. I'm talking about Indo-China."

"The Far East? The French, they've left, they. . ."

"We are replacing them" she said.

"Really? How do you know that?"

"It's my job to know" she said. "What I am saying is that if you're headed for Germany, you're going in the wrong direction."

Apparently she had found what she was looking for in her briefcase. A sheet of paper. An invitation, it looked like, as Dee glanced down to see what she had.

She read it, put it in her purse, and then, after a pause, said "Isn't that the Governor's mansion on the left? Yes, it is, so if you will pull into that parking place you can drop me there."

As she got out she looked at him and said "Thanks for the ride, and good luck, Lieutenant Dee. We'll keep the home fires burning."

She has an odd sense of humor, whoever the hell she is, Dee said softly, to himself, as he got out of the car and walked across the street to the fenced in dog run area on the governor's lawn.

The Valdez Memorial Dog Run, according to a small sign on the fence. Herman had told him about it, how the police maintain the area, how Hattie pays them once a month to do that, using the fund left behind by that old man with the seeing eye dog.

The rich old man who died in Ginger's arms that night at Hattie's. Spelling it out in his will, leaving behind a small fortune for a dog run on the governor's lawn. And Hattie, somehow persuading the governor to allow it.

Hattie Valdez. But they wouldn't dare call it Hattie's Dog Run. No way.

"I remember you now" said someone on the other side of the fence as Dee walked along the edge. The man with the badly scarred face, who had stopped at the clearing on the road into Austin, across from the vacant area where the Pink House had been located.

"Right" said Dee. "You were wondering how I could afford a Cadillac."

"No" he replied. "It's not that."

"Your name" said Dee. What's your name?"

"Langley" the man answered. "August Langley."

"So what is it you remember, Mister Langley?"

"Five years ago, that picture of you in the paper, with that headline about your being castrated, that's what I finally remembered."

"What does that mean, castrated?" asked the little girl with him, still holding their dog. "Does that mean he's been drinking castor oil?"

"No, little sister" said Langley. "That's not what it means, so take Boris for a walk while I talk with this lieutenant."

"Whatever it means, that headline wasn't true" said Dee.

"I can see that" said Langley. "Hell, you must be on your way to general now,"

"General? What are you talking about?"

"That lady who was with you, that's what I'm talking about."

"Her? What about her? I don't even know her name" said Dee.

As he spoke Langley watched the woman walking to the entrance to the governor's mansion. Dee also watched as she pressed the doorbell and disappeared inside after handing a butler a card, no doubt the one she had taken from her briefcase.

"She had an invitation" said Dee.

"Invitation, hell" said Langley. "It's Little Rock all over again."

"I can't keep up with you" said Dee. "One second you're talking about being a general, the next second it's Little Rock, damn, I. . ."

"She's the assistant Sec Def" said Langley. "You didn't know that?"

"The Assistant Secretary of Defense? Her? Hell no, I. . ."

"She's Eisenhower's big gun, he uses her to push the laws on integration."

"Little Rock, then . . . she's the one who. . ."

"Central High" said Langley. "She's the one who brought in that battalion from the Hundred and First Airborne, to integrate that school."

"How do you know all this?" asked Dee. "How did you recognize her?"

Langley was silent for a moment, watching the young girl he calls "Little Sister" chasing her dog. The dog named Boris. Everybody has a name. Except for this woman he gave a ride to. She doesn't need a name. Not her. That title is enough.

"We were together on a panel" said Langley.

"A panel? That's how you recognized her?"

"We were testifying before a Senate committee."

"The Senate, you were there about integration? Sure, I. . ."

"Not about integration. About military decorations."

"Decorations, then you. . ."

"This afternoon, I think you said you're on your way to Germany."

"I am, but I'm not taking that Cadillac with me."

"Fine, and I'll give you some advice. Stay away from Korea."

"Korea, sure, but. . ."

"That's where I got this face."

Dee watched as Langley took the dog leash from Little Sister, who had returned with Boris. As he started to walk away with Boris Dee noticed once again the scar on Langley's face, how ugly it was. No wonder he sounded so bitter.

"My uncle told me you're a paratrooper" said Little Sister.

"I am" said Dee.

"If there's another war, maybe you can win the Medal of Honor too."

"Your uncle, he got that medal in Korea, did he?"

"He did, and when you win it you can come back and give me a hug."

"A hug. I'll remember that."

"Just don't get your face so messed up. I might not like you then."

Dee reached over the fence, patted her on the head, and said he promised her he would take care of his face. As he walked to his car he looked up the sky. All clear, nothing but stars, no need to put the top up.

"So we're off to Germany" he said out loud. "But not Korea. Maybe Indo-China, if that Sec Def lady is right."

He started the engine and waited until the oil gauge needle lined up just right. And then, as he drove away, still out loud it was "Germany, Indo-China, hell, let it rip. Whichever way the wind blows."

About S.R. Doss:

S.R. Doss has been a journalist, a paratrooper, and a professor of philosophy. *Hattie's Pink House*, a novel about his earlier adventures as a newspaper reporter, is to be published next.

Made in the USA
Middletown, DE
17 February 2022

61315783R00123